PROJECT VRIKSHARA

GOKUL SURENDRAN

Cover design by : Akhilandeswary @a_kh_i_la_

Special Thanks: To *Saheeda M. Muhammed* – like a sister to me, whose support helped bring this book to life.

Edited by : Gokul Surendran

First Edition – 2025

ISBN: 978-93-344-2134-7

Genre: Science Fiction | Mystery | Thriller

For updates on upcoming books and projects, follow the author on Instagram: **@super_gokul**

To Ammukutty & Sreekutty

To whom I shall always be grateful for her friendship and the encouragement she gave me all these years.

CHAPTER 1

Death in Kallukad

The phone rang–thin as a blade through the quiet of evening. John Thomas lifted his eyes from the worn leather chair and the cup of tea cooling in his hands. Through the cracked window drifted the faint sweetness of hibiscus. He hadn't had a call all day.

He reached for the phone.

"John Thomas?" a voice asked – young, frail, hesitant.

"Yes."

"My name is Varun. I saw your number in a newspaper ad. I... I need help. Can I come over?"

John glanced at the fading light outside. The tea had lost its warmth. "Come. I'll be here."

***

The next morning, John was in his garden, pruning jasmine vines along the rusted fence, when an autorickshaw rumbled to a stop at the gate. A young man climbed out—dusty blue jeans, a brown shirt, a faded backpack slung over one shoulder. There was something in his eyes, something hollow, like a scream trapped behind silence.

"Hi, I'm Varun. Isn't this Mr. John's office?"

"It is. Come in."

As the gate creaked open, John found himself guessing—an old habit. Lost dog? Runaway wife? Misplaced gold chain? Cases these days were dull enough to put a corpse to sleep.

"I'm the one who called yesterday," Varun said.

"I remember. Office is that way." John pointed to the repurposed tool shed at the back. "Give me a minute."

John washed his face, buttoned a fresh shirt, and stepped in—just in time to see Varun halfway out the door.

"Sorry," Varun muttered. "I'm leaving."

John's brows drew together. "Is this a joke?"

Varun paused, gaze drifting to a sepia-toned photograph on the wall: John in full uniform, back straight, medals gleaming.

"I didn't know you were police," he said quietly. "They never help people like me."

John stepped forward, blocking the doorway. "Sit down, Varun."

After a moment's hesitation, Varun sank into the chair across the desk, fingers tight on his backpack straps.

Inside, the shed still smelled of old paper and rust. A kettle steamed gently on a hotplate beside a cluttered desk. John poured tea and slid a cup across.

"Yes, I was a cop," John said. "Thirty years with the Kerala Police. Retired two years ago. Now I work for people who have nowhere else to go."

Varun nodded, eyes fixed on the steam. "Sorry. The police never helped me. That's why I'm here. Can you help me? Can I trust you?"

"That depends. Are you ready to tell me the truth?"

He swallowed, then took a careful sip. "Yes."

"Then let's start with your story."

"My name's Varun. I'm from Kallukad, in Idukki. I run a small newspaper delivery business. My case... it's strange. No one believes me."

He unzipped the backpack and drew out a folded newspaper, its edges soft with handling. "This was three months ago."

Idukki—that's a long way from here, John thought.

He took the paper. The headline screamed: **TIGER ATTACK IN IDUKKI – ONE DEAD**

He raised an eyebrow. Tiger attacks weren't uncommon in forest-bordering villages, but something in Varun's tone didn't match the usual tragedy.

"It wasn't a tiger," Varun said.

"Why do you think that?"

"Because I was the first one there."

"Go on," John said, leaning forward.

"It was about nine at night," Varun began. "I was riding my bike along the forest road when I heard a cry—a human cry—from the right. I thought maybe a drunk had fallen. I used my torch and saw something move. I parked the bike and walked slowly through the trees."

He stopped, the memory lodging in his throat.

"And then... I saw the body. Torn apart. Legs here, arms there—the head—" He drew a breath. "The body wasn't mauled. It was detached. I collapsed. I couldn't scream. Couldn't move. Just blood. Everywhere."

John's gaze stayed steady. "You called the police?"

"There was no one in the forest. I shouted, but no one answered," Varun said. "So I went to the station and reported it. Only then did they come."

His expression hardened. “When they returned the body to me, they said it was a tiger attack—that there were claw marks. But that’s a lie. I saw the body first. There were no claw marks.”

“They returned the body to you?” John asked.

Varun’s eyes clouded. “It was my father.”

The words landed with weight. John sat back. “I’m sorry.”

“He raised me alone. My mother died when I was young. He was everything to me.”

Varun pulled a battered file from his backpack and laid it carefully on the desk.

“These are the post-mortem and police reports,” he said. “They both say tiger attack. But it’s wrong, sir. I was there. I know what I saw.”

John flipped through the pages. Every line, every stamp, every signature looked official. Too official.

“Did they find the tiger?” he asked.

"They claimed there were tracks. But I didn't see any. The blood was undisturbed. No drag marks. No signs of a struggle."

"Who saw him last?"

"His friends. They'd been drinking. He left around eight-thirty."

"And the police?"

"They shut the case in two days. No follow-ups."

John tapped his pen on the pad. "Did your father have enemies?"

Varun shook his head. "No. Everyone liked him."

"And the villagers? How did they react?"

"They started avoiding me," Varun said, voice dropping. "Some tried to convince me it was a tiger. They think I'm mad."

"You've been through something terrible," John said. "Grief can bend memory. But I need to ask—are you certain about what you saw?"

"I've replayed it a thousand times," Varun said. "I'm sure."

John nodded once. “Then I believe you. But belief isn’t enough. We need evidence.”

He opened a fresh page in his notebook. “Tell me about your father.”

“Prabakaran,” Varun said, a faint smile flickering. “A rubber tapper. Cheerful. Kind. Helped everyone.”

“Education?”

“Pre-degree. Worked in Chennai for a while, then came back. Said he missed home.”

“His friends—what do they say about the incident?”

“They believe it was a tiger.”

“Any issues with them? Old grudges?”

“No. Childhood friends.”

“Village politics? Fights? Feuds?”

“None. He stayed away from trouble.”

“Did he mention seeing anything strange the days before his death?”

“Never.”

John scribbled. "This happened on November twenty-second?"

Varun nodded.

"The post-mortem confirms an animal attack," John said, scanning the report. "But if it was a tiger... why didn't it drag the body away? Predators don't leave fresh kills."

"Exactly," Varun said. "Something's wrong."

"Did the police collect fur, hair, droppings?"

"They said they found tracks. But the blood was undisturbed. No struggle. No trail."

"Who led the investigation?"

"Sub-Inspector Krishnankutty. He closed it fast. Two days. Done."

"And the Forest Department?"

"They also gave the tiger story."

"Did anyone actually see this tiger?"

"No one."

John leaned back, the weight of the file heavy in his hands. The pieces refused to fall into place. Either someone had gone to great lengths to bury the truth, or Varun's grief had twisted what he remembered. But one thing was certain: something didn't add up.

"We have a dead man," John murmured, "last seen by his friends, discovered by his son. The supposed killer is a tiger no one saw—and it left the kill behind."

Varun's hands tightened on the desk. "I just want someone to believe me."

"I do," John said. "Now we find proof."

A flicker of hope touched Varun's face. His shoulders eased, just slightly.

John turned to the window. The jasmine vines stirred in the breeze, whispering secrets only the wind could carry.

"We start with your village," he said. "Kallukad. I need to see the scene. Talk to people."

"I'll take you," Varun said. "Whenever you're ready."

John gave a firm nod.

"Then let's find out what really happened

CHAPTER 2

Trip to Kallukad

The evening sun cast long shadows across the quiet room as John packed his bag. He slid in his 9mm pistol, a precaution he rarely took lightly. This wasn't going to be a simple case. Varun's words lingered in his mind: the certainty in his voice, the unease behind his eyes, the quiet fear he tried to mask. Whether it was grief distorting the truth or something far more sinister, John knew one thing. Something didn't add up. And Kallukad was where the answers waited.

Before leaving, John pulled out his smartphone and ran a quick search on Kallukad. The village, it turned out, was spread across an area of roughly 203 square kilometers, most of it covered in dense forest. Only about fifty families lived there, scattered among the hills and trees. The village had a small police station, a quiet junction with a few stores, a handful of temples, and sprawling fields of rubber, cardamom, and black pepper. A remote, tightly-knit world. The kind of place where everyone knew each other and where secrets could linger in silence for years.

"I bet Varun's father's death was the most interesting thing that had happened here in a long time," John muttered to himself, his eyes scanning the map.

He also ran a search for *Tiger attacks in Kallukad.* Only two news reports appeared. One was about Varun's father, recent, grim, and sparse on details. The other was from nearly a year ago: another man, named Sathish, had been killed in what was also labeled a tiger attack.

John leaned back in his chair, eyes narrowing as thoughts tangled in his mind.

What if Varun is wrong? he wondered. *Who would go to the trouble of killing a man like his father, a quiet, working-class nobody, and then stage it to look like a tiger attack?*

What if it really was the same tiger from the old report?

But the doubt didn't settle.

What if Varun is right? I've seen liars before, eyes shifting, voices cracking, but Varun wasn't one of them. He believed every word he said. But belief and truth weren't always the same. Grief can twist a man's memories, bend them into safer shapes. I've seen that too. Maybe he just can't face the loss. Maybe his mind created a mystery so he wouldn't have to accept the silence..

John sighed, zipped his bag, and rose to his feet.

"Only one way to be sure," he muttered, fastening the worn strap of his Casio F91W around his wrist.

He stepped outside and called out, "Varun. Let's go. It's getting dark."

***

By the time they left John's home, twilight had faded into the cool hush of night. John and Varun boarded a long-distance bus to Idukki, its old frame rattling as they settled into their seats.

The steady hum of the engine and the gentle sway of the road created a strange rhythm beneath their conversation, setting the tone for the long journey ahead.

"Tell me more about the night it happened," John said, breaking the silence. Varun stared out the window, his face catching the faint glow of passing streetlights, shadows flickering across his expression.

"I told you most of it, sir," he replied, his voice low, as if afraid the night itself might be listening. "But what still haunts me is the silence. After I saw the body, there was nothing. No animals. No insects. Just... silence."

John made a mental note of his observation. Forests are rarely silent at night. That's something you learn quickly in this line of work. When nature falls quiet, it usually means something isn't right. Something unnatural.

"What were your father's daily routines like?" John asked.

Varun thought for a moment before replying. "He usually woke up very early to go tapping. He'd have food from the estate itself. By noon, he'd be back home and take a nap around this time. Later, he'd head to the junction and stop by my shop. Then he'd buy some meat or fish for dinner and head back. On the way, he'd meet his friends and chat for a while. After that, he'd go home and cook dinner before I got back. On some days, he'd come home late, he'd be out drinking with his friends."

As the bus trudged along the winding mountain roads, Varun spoke more about his father, his personality, the kind of man he was, and how the village of Kallukad had changed over the years. He painted a picture of a quiet place, where everyone knew each other.

"My father always said Kallukad was a peaceful place," Varun said. "But after his death, it feels... different."

"You said people have been avoiding you?" John asked, keeping his tone even. "Anyone in particular?"

"Not really," Varun replied, shaking his head. "It's more like everyone. Even those who were close to my father. It's like they think I've lost my mind since he died."

John nodded, filing away the details. The more he listened, the more it became clear to him this wasn't just a case of a questionable death. There were layers beneath the surface, and he was only beginning to uncover them.

The hours passed in a blur of dimly lit roads and brief halts at Idukki bus station. At 4:30 AM, the bus came to a slow, weary stop, and they stepped out into the crisp, silent air of pre-dawn.

"This is Idukki town," Varun said.

"I've been here before," John replied, adjusting his backpack.

"Oh? When was that?" Varun asked, curiosity in his tone.

"I don't remember the year exactly. It was for a case I investigated," John said, his gaze drifting across the still-sleeping town.

"We'll have to wait for the bus to Kallukad. It leaves at 5 a.m.," Varun added, pointing to an old bus parked near the station.

"Let's get some tea while we wait," John said. "I'm feeling a bit tired."

They drifted toward a roadside tea stall, the morning chill nipping at their skin. The owner was still arranging cups and kettles, the day only just beginning. Soon, they found a place on a rough wooden bench. The first sip of hot, fragrant tea sent warmth seeping into their hands, their chests, pushing back the cold silence that clung to Idukki's dawn.

"So... what do you think about my case?" Varun asked.

"To be honest, I don't know, Varun," John replied. "In cases like this, there's always a motive and a means. But as you said, your father was a pretty normal man, with no known enemies. So who would have a reason to kill him and the ability to make it look like a tiger attack?"

Varun silently sipped his tea. "I know it doesn't make a lot of sense, sir. That's why I came to you."

John nodded slightly, watching the steam rise from his cup. "Do you know someone named Sathish? He was also killed by a tiger."

"Yes," Varun said, looking up. "It happened about a year ago, near the border of our area. The forest officers captured the tiger sometime after that."

"What happened to it? Do you know?"

"I think it was released near the Periyar Tiger Reserve. That's a long way from my village. Do you think it could be the same tiger?"

John shook his head slightly. "Can't be sure. The forest department should have records." He paused, finishing the last sip of his tea. "I'll have to make a few calls."

Varun leaned forward, his eyes intense. "Believe me, sir. It wasn't a tiger attack. I'm sure of it."

John met his gaze, steady and calm. "I believe you, Varun. But belief isn't enough. We need evidence. The police reports, the postmortem findings, everything points the other way. We'll get to the bottom of this. Just be patient."

A sharp blast from a bus horn cut through the quiet, ending their conversation.

"That's our bus. It's about to leave," Varun said, already getting to his feet.

***

They boarded quickly and found seats by the window. The bus was nearly empty, the quiet hum of its engine soon becoming the only sound around them. Varun bought the tickets while John settled in, adjusting his bag and glancing out the window.

As the bus pulled out of the station, it rolled through the last stretch of town before veering into the forested hills. The scenery changed swiftly: deep green valleys opened up on one side, waterfalls cascaded down mossy cliffs on the other. Towering trees lined the road, casting long shadows across the winding path.

John leaned back and let the scenes wash over him. Even with the weight of the case on his mind, he couldn't help but admire the haunting beauty of Idukki's wilderness.

After a few minutes winding through dense forest roads, a weathered sign came into view: **Welcome to Kallukad.** Both John and Varun exchanged a quiet glance, a shared sense of arrival settling between them.

The bus continued its slow crawl through the thick canopy before rolling into a small junction. The place was hushed, wrapped in the kind of stillness only early morning can offer. A row of shuttered shops stood like silent sentinels along the empty street, their edges blurred by the soft glow of flickering street lamps. From somewhere nearby, faint strains of temple music drifted through the cool air, gentle, rhythmic, and hauntingly serene—the only sound to disturb the slumbering hour.

"This is Kallukad," Varun said, adjusting his bag with a tired shrug. His voice carried a strange mix of relief and unease, the kind that surfaces when returning to a place heavy with memory. Some memories, perhaps, offered comfort. Others did not. There was a quiet tension in him, just beneath the surface, as if stepping back here had awakened something he wasn't ready to face.

"Is your home near?" John asked, breaking the stillness.

"It's a little distance from here," Varun replied, nodding toward an old Yamaha RX100 parked near the edge of the road. "We can take my bike."

John raised an eyebrow, eyeing the scooter. "I'm impressed," he said. "If this were Trivandrum, that thing would have disappeared in ten minutes."

Varun let out a quiet chuckle, but the tension in his expression lingered. "We don't have theft in Kallukad," he said. "Not yet, anyway."

John nodded, quietly acknowledging the stark contrast, the quiet trust that lingered in this village, so different from the constant edge of vigilance that city life demanded.

Varun swung a leg over the bike and settled into the seat. John climbed on behind him. The engine sputtered to life, its growl cutting through the morning stillness. Before pulling away, Varun gestured toward a shuttered shop across the road.

"This was my shop, sir," Varun said, his voice tinged with nostalgia. "I used to run a newspaper agency here."

Varun's gaze lingered on the shuttered shop. "After the incident... I wasn't in a state to keep it going. I had to sell it."

John studied his face for a moment, catching the weight behind the words. The silence that followed was thick, filled only by the soft idle of the engine and the distant murmur of temple music still hanging in the air.

John gently patted Varun's back, signaling him to move on.

Varun gave the engine a soft rev, and the bike rolled forward, its tires crunching lightly over the gravel. They moved through the quiet lanes of the waking village, shadows retreating as the morning light stretched across Kallukad. Every turn of the road seemed to carry them deeper not just into the forested paths ahead, but into the heart of the mystery that had drawn them here.

As they rode on, the town slipped quietly behind them, replaced by the wide, hushed expanse of rural Kallukad. The road curved gracefully past a small temple nestled in a grove of trees, its tiled roof glowing in the morning light. A delicate trace of incense lingered in the crisp air, blending with the earthy scent of dew-soaked leaves. A few early devotees stood at the temple steps, hands folded in prayer, their faces serene in the gentle warmth of dawn. It was a scene of stillness and reverence, untouched by the troubles that rode with them.

They drove for nearly an hour, the road gradually shedding its smooth veneer. The asphalt faded into rutted dirt tracks, scattered with loose stones and lined by creeping undergrowth. With every turn, the path grew narrower, winding deeper into the forest where the trees stood tall and close, their branches forming a canopy that filtered the morning light into shifting patterns. The air grew cooler, rich with the damp, earthy scent of moss and soil. Behind them, the hum of village life disappeared entirely, replaced by the soft rustle of leaves and the distant cry of unseen birds echoing through the green silence.

"This is the way to my home," Varun said, his voice steady as the bike bumped along the narrowing path. "It's a bit remote."

John, seated behind him, glanced at the dense forest pressing in on either side. "I can tell," he replied dryly, gripping his bag a little tighter.

John scanned the towering trees pressing close on either side. The forest was dense, its silence unsettling, disturbed only by the faint rustle of leaves or the snap of a twig underfoot. A strange stillness clung to the air, as if they had slipped out of time and into a forgotten corner of the world. The road ahead had withered into a narrow, winding trail, swallowed by shadows where the canopy thickened and sunlight struggled to seep through. It felt as though Kallukad itself had closed around them, drawing them deeper into its silent, watchful heart.

"Quite the journey," John muttered, mostly to himself.

Varun didn't reply right away, but gave a quiet nod, his eyes locked on the path ahead. His silence wasn't dismissive, it was the kind that came from familiarity. He had taken this route many times before.

As they continued along the winding forest path, the air turned dense, almost weighty, thick with the scent of damp earth and foliage. The trees loomed overhead like silent sentinels, their branches arching above the road like a canopy of shadows. The path beneath the wheels grew rougher, strewn with fallen leaves and snapped twigs, each bump a reminder of how far removed they were from the world behind them.

John sat in silence, his thoughts drifting between the haunting beauty of the forest and the grim uncertainty of the case ahead. There was something about this place, the stillness, the depth that felt as if it were guarding secrets, buried beneath layers of time and silence. As the bike moved forward, he noticed a line of electric poles running alongside the path, their presence stark and jarring amidst the trees. They were the only sign of the modern world, stretching like a fragile thread through the heart of the wilderness. None of them had street lights, just bare poles.

Suddenly, Varun eased off the throttle, and the bike rolled to a gentle stop. The engine sputtered once before dying, its absence making the forest's silence feel louder, more alive. Only the rustle of leaves and the occasional call of a distant bird remained.

Varun's eyes scanned the trees, sharp and searching, as if expecting something or someone to emerge from the undergrowth. Then he turned to John. A pause hung between them, brief but weighted. In that silence, John caught it: a flicker of unease in Varun's expression, a tension that hadn't been there before.

It wasn't just a place they were nearing.

It was something more. Something that had already left a mark.

"This is the place," Varun said quietly, pointing toward a clearing on the right side of the road. His voice carried a hush, almost reverent, as if the ground itself demanded silence. "This is where it happened."

John followed Varun's gaze, his eyes sweeping over the overgrown patch of ground beside the road. The forest pressed in from both sides, dense and shadow-laden, the trees standing like silent witnesses. At first glance, the spot looked ordinary, just a bed of dirt, fallen leaves, and tangled undergrowth. But there was something in the stillness, something in the way the silence lingered here longer than it should. His instincts stirred. Whatever had happened that night had left its mark, even if it wasn't immediately visible.

John could feel the weight of the moment settle around them, as if the forest itself was holding its breath. The tension in Varun's posture, the quiet in his voice, it all pointed to something deeper, something unresolved. Whatever had happened here, it hadn't just left a mark on the ground. It had carved itself into Varun. John drew a slow, measured breath, letting the forest air fill his lungs. He needed clarity, focus. There was truth buried here, and he intended to dig it out.

"This is where it happened?" John asked, his voice low but steady. His instincts prickled with quiet urgency, something about the spot tugged at his gut, a subtle wrongness he couldn't quite name. He scanned the trees again, the undergrowth, the way the shadows clung a little too tightly to the ground. Something had happened here. And it wasn't finished telling its story.

Varun nodded slowly, his eyes clouded with a mixture of sorrow and dread. "Yes... this is where I found him. My father." His voice faltered slightly, but he quickly steadied himself, as if the words themselves caused a sharp pain.

John climbed off the bike, and Varun did the same. Without a word, Varun stepped forward, as though something unseen was pulling him toward the patch of earth. His movements were slow, deliberate, each footfall guided more by instinct than thought.

"I don't know what happened that night," he said quietly, his voice tinged with something between fear and certainty. "But I know it wasn't just a tiger attack. Something else happened here."

John scanned the area carefully, his eyes tracing the outlines of the forest floor, the way the undergrowth bowed in certain places, the subtle scars in the earth. He tried to reconstruct the chaos that must have erupted here, to imagine the final moments of a man's life in this silent place.

"Tell me everything," John urged, his voice gentle, but insistent. "The more details we have, the better chance we'll have of understanding what really happened here."

"It was right there." Varun pointed toward the right side of the path and began walking briskly in that direction. The spot he indicated wasn't far, only about ten meters off the trail. John followed closely behind.

When he stopped, his hand fell to his side, motioning toward the forest floor. The area was blanketed in a thick layer of dry leaves, and tall trees loomed in every direction, their branches casting long shadows that seemed to stretch endlessly.

Three months had passed since the incident, and John couldn't help but feel a twinge of doubt. Could anything of value still be found here, after so much time? The forest had a way of erasing traces, burying answers beneath layers of silence and decay. Still, it wouldn't hurt to look. Sometimes, even the smallest detail could crack a case wide open. He reminded himself of that as he stepped forward, eyes sharp, instincts alert.

John surveyed the area carefully. The spot was close to the dirt path, too close to be entirely overlooked, yet isolated enough to go unnoticed by a casual passerby. His gaze shifted to the trees encircling the area, searching for any scratches, marks, or signs of disturbance. But there was nothing. Just the undisturbed bark of ancient trunks, standing as silent witnesses to whatever had happened there.

John pulled out his smartphone and began taking photos, documenting everything he could. The stillness of the moment felt surreal, almost as if time had frozen in place, leaving only traces of what once was.

"I know you've told me everything," John said, his tone calm but probing. "But think carefully, are you sure there's nothing you might have forgotten to mention? Try to remember. Was this spot disturbed in any way? Any signs of a struggle here?"

Varun furrowed his brow, the wheels of his memory visibly turning. “It was dark,” he said hesitantly, then paused. Suddenly, something clicked. “But... the bike was there.”

Varun pointed toward the bike they had arrived on.

“This bike?” John asked.

Varun nodded, his expression heavy. “It was my father’s bike. I didn’t see it at first. After I called the police, I came back here and found it—crashed on the left side of the road. And that’s when it struck me... the body lying there was my father.”

John walked back to the dirt road, his eyes fixed on the bike. It stood there in the shadows, a silent witness to the events that had unfolded. It was an old Yamaha RX100, but despite its age, it was well-maintained. The chrome parts gleamed faintly in the sunlight, and the black paint had been kept pristine.

John crouched down to inspect the bike more closely. The left side of the fuel tank bore clear signs of impact: a few scuff marks and scratches, but nothing that screamed foul play. Still, the image of the bike, abandoned so carelessly on the side of the path, seemed to stick in his mind.

He snapped a few photos of the damage. "Where exactly was the bike when you saw it?" he asked, his voice calm but searching.

Varun pointed to the left side of the path. "Right here... it had fallen to the left side."

John scanned the ground around them, looking for any other clues. "Were there any other signs on the path? Any skid marks, brake marks?"

Varun nodded uncertainly. John gave him a reassuring look. "It's okay, it's been three months, right? Just let me know if anything else comes to mind."

Varun gave a small, uncertain nod in return, his gaze drifting as if he was still trying to piece together the fragments of that night.

"Where does this path lead, other than to your house?" John asked, trying to gather more details.

"After a few meters the path splits, one leads into the forest," he replied. "That path ends in the deep forest. The other one goes to our house, it also leads into the forest."

John glanced around. The trees pressed in on both sides, thick and quiet.

"Any houses nearby?" he asked.

Varun shook his head. "None around here."

"Is this the only route to your place?"

"It is," Varun replied. "No other way in or out."

"Then let's head to your home," John suggested.

***

They both climbed onto the bike, with Varun taking the lead as they headed toward his house. The road twisted through dense greenery, revealing the occasional scattered house, each set apart by stretches of wilderness. The area felt remote, untouched by the rush of modern life. There were no people in sight, only the silence of the forest pressing in from all sides. The stillness was broken only by the steady hum of the engine and the soft rustle of wind moving through the trees.

Varun brought the bike to a halt where the path split into two. He pointed toward the trail veering left.

"That way leads deep into the forest," he said quietly. "No houses there. People usually avoid it."

Then he gestured to the right.

"My house is this way."

John's eyes lingered on the left path, studying the dense shadows between the trees. There was something unsettling about its silence, something that made it hard to look away.

John gave Varun a reassuring pat on the back, signaling him to continue. Without a word, Varun turned the throttle and guided the bike down the right-hand path, the one leading toward his home.

After half a kilometer of twists and turns, the bike finally reached Varun's home, a modest house nestled beside the dirt road. A few other houses stood scattered nearby, quiet and still. Varun leaned forward, pushed open the creaking iron gate with the front wheel, and slowly drove the bike inside.

John got off the bike as Varun parked it beside an old scooter, its surface layered in dust. The house stood before them, whitewashed but unpainted, its walls showing signs of wear. The small garden out front looked neglected, some plants had withered from lack of care, while weeds had crept in, claiming whatever space they could find.

As Varun rummaged through his backpack for the keys, John took a slow look around. The morning air was still, heavy with the scent of damp earth and forest. From a neighboring house, a few curious faces peeked through half-open windows and doorways, their eyes quietly studying the unfamiliar visitor at Varun's gate. Their expressions held no malice, just the wary interest of a close-knit place where strangers seldom arrived unnoticed.

Varun unlocked the door and stepped inside.

"Come in, sir... please," he said quickly, his voice a little rushed as he hurried to gather the crumpled clothes scattered across the living room floor.

John stepped in behind him, taking in the modest interior. The house was small, just a living room, a narrow kitchen, two bedrooms, and a bathroom that, from the looks of it, was separate and located outside. The place had a lived-in feel, worn but honest, like everything here had a purpose and a history.

"This must be your father," John said, pausing in front of a framed photograph on the wall. His eyes lingered on the image, an older man with kind eyes and a quiet strength in his posture, frozen in time.

"Yes," Varun replied softly. "That's him."

He stepped closer, pointing to another photo just beside it.

"And that's him with my mother. It's the only picture I have of them together."

John studied the picture, sepia-toned, edges slightly curled, the kind that held silence in its grain. A moment frozen in time.

"What was her name?" he asked, his voice low.

"Geetha," Varun replied, a small, wistful smile tugging at his lips.

"How old were you when she passed?"

"I was really young," Varun said, eyes flicking briefly to the floor. "It was malaria."

John offered a faint smile as his eyes moved across the living room. An old television rested on a low wooden stand, its screen dulled with age. A few handmade chairs, fashioned from woven cane and sticks, were arranged loosely around the space. A modest dining table stood near the far wall, doubling the room's purpose without making it feel cramped. Despite the simplicity, and the wear that time had left behind, the space felt lived-in, humble, and quietly warm.

"I'm quite tired from the journey, Varun," John said, his voice carrying the weight of the long ride. "Do you have a place where I can rest for a while?"

"Of course. You can use this room," Varun replied, gesturing to the first door on the left.

John picked up his bag and stepped inside. The room was noticeably cleaner than the rest of the house, tidy, though a light film of dust lingered on the surfaces. Everything else, from the neatly folded bed sheet to the carefully placed books on the side table, felt untouched, preserved.

He set his bag down and turned to Varun.

"I'm guessing this was your father's room?" John asked gently.

Varun looked slightly taken aback, then nodded. "Yes... How did you know?"

John gave a faint smile. "It's obvious. Everything in here feels preserved."

He set his bag down by the bed and stretched his shoulders. "Let me get some rest. We'll talk later, alright?"

"Of course, sir," Varun said. "I'll rest too. After that, we can have something to eat."

"Well, that's a plan," John said.

Varun stepped out, pulling the door gently shut behind him. John placed his bag on the floor, changed into something more comfortable, folded the used one over the back of a chair, and dusted the bed with deliberate, tired motions. The cot creaked as he lowered himself onto it, the mattress thin but passable.

He pulled out his phone and began scrolling through the photos he'd taken earlier at the forest trail, branches and patches of dry leaves. Nothing jumped out. Just the forest floor caught in poor lighting and shadows.

With a quiet sigh, he plugged in the phone to charge, set it on the side table, and lay back. The fan overhead turned slowly, humming like a tired old song. John closed his eyes, letting the rhythm guide him toward sleep, though the weight of questions still lingered in the dark.

CHAPTER 3

Vana Sundari

John woke with a start, the remnants of a shallow nap slipping away like mist. He sat up and instinctively glanced at his wristwatch. **10:00 AM.** He had slept longer than intended.

Knock. Knock.

Firm. Repeated. Coming from the front door.

He rose, blinking the drowsiness from his eyes. The house was quiet except for the knocking.

Knock. Knock.

“Varun,” a voice called—soft but urgent.

John stepped out of the room, still adjusting to the light, and opened the door. A young girl stood just outside, a large tiffin box in one hand and a kettle in the other. She paused, brow furrowed with curiosity as her eyes scanned him. Her long, dark curls framed her face, untamed but striking, giving her an energy that contrasted sharply with the quiet morning.

"You must be Praba uncle's friend. Varun said something about..."

Before John could reply, Varun appeared behind him, hair still tousled from sleep.

"Yes... yes, this is Dad's friend from Trivandrum," he said quickly, tone casual, almost too casual.

The girl gave him a sharp look before turning back to John with a small smile.

"Uncle, this is Priya, our neighbor," Varun explained, rubbing the back of his neck. "And this is John uncle."

John nodded politely. "Nice to meet you, Priya."

He barely got the words out before she brushed past Varun and stepped inside as if the house already belonged to her.

"You know, uncle, this guy nearly gave me a heart attack," she said, setting the tiffin and kettle on the dining table. "Didn't open the door, didn't answer... I thought he'd run off or something."

John chuckled softly, watching the exchange with quiet amusement. There was warmth in her scolding—the kind reserved for people who mattered.

Varun pulled out his worn wallet, counted a few folded notes, and handed them to her.

"Here... last month's food bill," he said, offering 1500 rupees.

"Thanks," Priya replied with a quick smile, tucking the money into her pocket. She turned to John, curiosity flickering in her eyes.

"You didn't tell me you had a visitor," she said, narrowing her gaze at Varun. "I'll bring food for him too. Just wait."

And before either man could respond, she was already halfway out the gate.

John watched her leave, then turned to Varun with a raised eyebrow.

Varun exhaled and dropped into a cane chair. “She runs a small catering business,” he explained.

There was a pause. John’s expression didn’t shift.

Varun gave a faint, embarrassed chuckle. “People here think I’ve lost it, sir. That’s why I told her you were a friend of my dad’s... not a detective.”

John nodded slowly. “Sometimes,” he said, “it’s easier to chase the truth when no one’s watching.”

Varun smiled faintly.

“I’ll freshen up,” John said.

He stepped into his room for a towel and toiletry bag, then headed outside to the detached bathroom. The air was crisp, carrying the earthy scent of damp soil and distant trees. After a quick wash and change of clothes, he returned to the hall.

A second tiffin box now sat neatly on the dining table. Priya was gone. The house felt quieter without her vibrant presence.

Varun entered from the opposite room, also freshly dressed, hair damp.

"Looks like Priya dropped off food for both of us," John said, gesturing toward the tiffin.

Varun nodded, and they sat down together. The comforting clink of metal lids filled the silence as they opened the boxes.

Inside: a smaller container of thick, bright-red tomato chutney, and beneath the lid, a neat stack of steaming hot idlis, soft and fluffy.

The aroma hit John immediately—earthy, tangy, comforting. His mouth watered. He broke off a piece of idli, dipped it generously in chutney, and took a bite.

"Mmm..." he murmured. "Priya is a very good cook."

Varun smiled. "She is. Honestly, it's the only thing that's kept me fed properly these last few months."

John gave him a sideways glance, teasing. “So... she your girlfriend?”

Varun nearly choked on his idli. “No... no,” he said quickly, far too quickly. “She’s just a friend.”

“Alright, alright,” John said with a chuckle. “Just asking. She was scolding you a little too lovingly, that’s all.”

Varun laughed, rubbing his neck. “She’s always been like that.”

John reached for his phone. “After we eat, I need to make a few calls.”

“Calls about what?” Varun asked.

“Our first suspect,” John replied, voice steady. “The man-eating tiger they caught last year.”

“I think I still have his number,” he muttered, scrolling even as he ate another bite.

Varun leaned forward, his voice low but firm. “Sir... believe me, it wasn’t a tiger.”

John nodded slowly. “I know, Varun. You don’t want to believe a tiger did it. But we have to be sure. We need to tick all the boxes.”

CHAPTER 4

Lady in the woods

John finished his meal in silence and stepped over to the small sink to wash his hands. A few minutes later, he returned and settled back into the chair, pulling out his phone.

Varun kept eating, but his eyes lingered on John with quiet curiosity.

John tapped a contact and lifted the phone to his ear. The call rang once... twice...

"Hi, it's John," he said, leaning back.

A pause. Then his tone shifted, words careful, measured.

"There was a tiger attack about a year ago near Kallukad, in Idukki. The tiger was captured. I want to know what happened to it—can you check the records for me?"

Another pause. John nodded slightly.

"Thanks, Rahul. No, nothing serious. Just a personal project. Call me back when you have it."

He ended the call with a soft tap.

Varun looked up from his last bite of idli, hope flickering in his eyes.

"Well?"

"That was Rahul," John said. "He works with the forest department. He'll check the records and get back to me later."

Varun nodded slowly, though tension still pressed on his shoulders. "Okay."

John leaned forward. "Where can we meet your father's friends?"

"They'll be at work now. By evening they'll be back."

"You mentioned they used to drink together. Where did that happen? Someone's house?"

Varun shook his head. "No... near the old Kavu. That's where they gathered."

John stood, slipping his phone into his pocket. "Let's go."

Varun blinked, surprised, then nodded. "Alright. It's a bit far."

"Doesn't matter," John said, already heading for the door.

Varun hurried to finish, washed his hands, and followed. He wheeled the bike from the yard as John climbed on behind him.

The engine sputtered to life. From across the lane, Priya stood in her doorway, her face shadowed with quiet worry. Varun didn't notice her. John did, but said nothing.

The bike rumbled back down the forest road, the trees swallowing them once again.

***

They retraced the winding path from that morning. The patch of roadside where Varun had first pointed out the crime scene slipped past. John turned his head, scanning the undergrowth again. It looked ordinary—just shadows and leaves—but the air still felt wrong.

He checked his watch. **11:00 AM.**

The deeper they rode, the thicker the canopy grew, dimming even the midday light. It wasn't shade—it was a darkness that swallowed the sun.

Varun eased off the throttle and stopped near a bend. He gestured toward a narrow passage disappearing into the forest. The trail was half-hidden by vines and fallen leaves, but signs of use were clear: footprints pressed into soft earth, branches snapped at shoulder height.

"We have to go this way," he said quietly.

John climbed off, eyes narrowing as he studied the path.

"At the end is an old abandoned Kavu," Varun said. "That's where they gather to drink."

John glanced at his watch. **11:25 AM.**

"That's nearly half an hour from where the body was found."

Varun nodded. "They said he left here around 8:30."

"And you found the body at nine," John murmured. "Postmortem confirms the same."

He exhaled slowly. "So either something fast and brutal happened in those thirty minutes... or his killers knew exactly when and where to strike."

***

The forest path narrowed. Varun pushed forward with the ease of familiarity. John followed close, his boots crunching softly over the leaves, eyes scanning every shadow.

After several minutes, the trees opened into a small clearing. Logs had been dragged into a circle, makeshift seating. Empty bottles, cigarette butts, rusted cans, plastic wrappers—the ghosts of many nights lingered here.

"This is where they drank?" John asked.

Varun nudged a bottle with his foot. "Almost every night. For years."

"And your father was here the night he died?"

"Yes. They said he left around 8:30."

John studied the clearing. "They don't come here now?"

"I'm not sure," Varun admitted. "I haven't spoken to them much since."

"Any houses nearby?"

Varun hesitated. "No... but there is one. An old woman lives alone, deep in the forest. People call her Puthana Ammumma. They say she's mad. Some even believe she practices black magic."

John raised an eyebrow. "Puthana—as in the demoness from the old tales?"

Varun gave a nervous chuckle. "Exactly. No one goes near her shack."

John's gaze turned toward the shadows. "Maybe it's time someone did."

***

They pressed deeper. Soon the trees thinned, revealing a mossy clearing.

An abandoned Kavu stood solemn, old stone idols of serpents nestled beneath a sacred tree, half-swallowed by roots. Some lay toppled, as though time itself had claimed them.

Varun pointed to a wisp of smoke curling above the trees. "She lives near here."

They followed the smoke until a crooked shack came into view, patched with tin and weathered wood. Smoke drifted from a crude chimney.

"I think this is it," Varun whispered.

Before John could answer, a thin, creaky voice floated out:

"I think I have some visitors..."

The wooden door opened. An old woman emerged, draped in a black saree, frail but sharp-eyed. A wide smile stretched across her face—too warm, too knowing.

"Ah... strangers in the forest," she said. "Not something I see every day."

Varun stiffened.

Her gaze lingered on John, as if looking through him, before she gestured toward a rough wooden bench.

"Come. The forest doesn't like people standing still too long."

Varun hesitated but sat. John remained standing a moment, scanning the shack and its scattered herbs, rusted vessels, hanging bundles. Then he joined.

“What shall I bring you—tea?” she asked, her smile grandmotherly yet edged with something sharper.

“No thanks,” John said gently. “We’re here to ask a few questions. I’m John. This is Varun.”

The woman’s eyes moved to Varun. “You’re Prabakaran’s son. The one who died.”

Varun stiffened. “You knew my father?”

“I know everyone here,” she said softly. “But they don’t remember me.”

John leaned forward. “Did you ever see or hear anything unusual that night?”

“I saw them often. I warned them not to defile this sacred land with bottles. But they never listened.”

John pressed. “Any arguments? Any trouble?”

She laughed, a dry, sly sound. "If you're doubting his friends killed him—no, Mister Policeman. They didn't."

Varun blinked. "How did you—?"

John frowned. "How do you know I'm police?"

"I had a doubt," she said, eyes twinkling. "Now I'm sure. John."

Her laugh was unsettling, amused by some private joke.

John studied her sharply. This woman, dismissed by villagers as mad, was no fool.

"So who killed him?" he asked.

"The forest," she said. "The forest killed him."

Her voice lowered, almost reverent.

"She's alive, Mr. John. She sees, she breathes, and sometimes... she takes. A life here, a soul there. To balance what we disturb."

She gestured toward a ritual space beside her shack. Flowers, turmeric, clay lamps flickering before a crude wooden idol. Green shoots sprouted from its surface like living veins.

"This is her," the woman whispered. "The one who watches. The one who remembers."

John stayed silent, eyes fixed on the living idol.

Varun muttered, "Like I said, sir... waste of time."

John nodded slowly, choosing not to challenge her belief. "Well... it was nice talking to you, Miss...?"

The woman smiled. "Parvathy. My name is Parvathy."

"Thank you, Miss Parvathy," John said politely.

As they left, her voice followed through the trees:

"The forest watches, Mr. John. You will see her soon."

***

John gave Parvathy a brief wave as they turned away from the shack. Her smile lingered behind them like the scent of smoke in the air.

They passed the old Kavu, the stone idols of snakes half-buried in moss and silence. Their steps carried them past the clearing where Varun's father and his friends once gathered—empty now, but still echoing with ghosts of laughter and clinking bottles.

As they neared the road where the bike was parked, John broke the quiet.

"Right," he muttered. "A man-eating forest goddess. Makes perfect sense."

Varun shook his head, pushing aside a low branch. "I told you, sir, she's nuts."

John didn't reply. His smile faded as his gaze wandered once more into the shadows.

"Let's head to the crime scene," he said, checking his watch. **12:15.**

"It should take us about half an hour. Did your father usually ride fast?"

"No. Thirty, forty at most."

"Then drive like he would have. Let's go."

They climbed onto the bike. With the forest pressing in from both sides, Varun started the engine and eased them forward.

The forest blurred past in shades of green and shadow. John's mind lingered on the old woman's words

The forest killed him...

He let out a faint breath, half amused.

"A forest god taking a life—impossible. But then again, when you've eliminated the impossible, whatever remains, however improbable, must be the truth."

The wind whipped past. But in John's mind, the case had just opened into stranger territory.

***

Varun slowed the bike, veering left. He eased off the throttle.

"We're here," he said quietly.

John checked his watch. **12:42.** Almost exactly half an hour.

They climbed off. The forest stood still, thick and watchful, as if holding its breath.

John stepped closer to the edge of the road, scanning the undergrowth with narrowed eyes. The crime scene waited somewhere beyond the trees, silent, hidden, but not forgotten.

"Where did you find the bike?" John asked.

"Here." Varun pointed left.

John crouched, studying the undergrowth and soil. "Can you place it how you saw it that night?"

Varun wheeled the bike forward and tilted it to the ground, mimicking the angle.

John crouched beside it, eyes sharp. "No impact marks. He wasn't hit. Which means he stopped—saw something—and fell."

He looked up. "No drag marks either?"

"None. The ground was untouched."

John stood slowly. "Then he wasn't taken. He walked in on his own. Willingly. Or... drawn."

They moved off the path into the undergrowth. When they reached the spot, they stopped.

John stood still for a long moment, letting the silence settle around him. Then he turned and looked at Varun, his gaze sharp, thoughtful.

"If you don't mind..." John began, hesitating just slightly. "Can you show me how the body was found?"

Varun took a deep breath, his shoulders tensing as old memories resurfaced. "Yes, sir."

"His torso was here. One leg here. Another there. One hand... there. The other... beside that tree. His head—right there."

John stayed silent, letting the weight of the memory hang in the air. He patted Varun's shoulder.

"Thanks."

The forest was impossibly still, listening.

***

"You said you fell backward here?" John asked.

"Yes. I tripped on a root and went down."

"And then?"

Varun swallowed. "I froze. Seconds, maybe minutes. Then I got up... went back to him. I saw his shirt. Torn, soaked, but his. I shone my torch on his face and knew—it was my father. I wanted to scream, but nothing came out. I just shook."

John's voice was gentle. "And then?"

"I called out to him. No response. I swept my torch around, but it flickered and died. I panicked. I ran back to the bike, rode to the station as fast as I could."

"Why not call?"

"My phone was dead. I didn't check. I just rode."

"And you brought the police back here?"

"Yes. They followed me. Locals gathered later."

John's eyes narrowed. "You know what that means, Varun? If the postmortem puts his death around nine... then the killer was still here. Watching. Hiding. And they chose not to kill you."

Varun turned instinctively, scanning the shadows.

John's gaze followed. "That's what unsettles me. Whoever—or whatever—it was, they let you walk away."

***

"You said the body was already torn apart when you saw it?" John pressed.

Varun nodded. "Yes. Ripped."

John's tone dropped, grim. "That kind of dismemberment isn't human. Not without tools. In the old days they used torture racks, horses pulling bodies apart. And here... it was done fast. Quiet. No screams. No struggle."

Varun's whisper trembled. "Then what could do that?"

John didn't answer. Because he wasn't sure it was a person at all.

He scanned the treetops, voice low. "Varun, is it possible you mistook it? In shock? Maybe... maybe it really was a tiger."

Varun's jaw tightened. "If you don't believe me, sir, you're welcome to leave. I'll pay your fare back to Trivandrum. No hard feelings. But I'll find the truth myself."

He swung onto the bike, engine roaring to life.

John stood still, then walked forward and placed a firm hand on his shoulder.

"Son, I don't think you're lying. If I did, I wouldn't be here. But I have to consider every angle. Sometimes the mind fills in blanks with fear. I'm here to find the truth. The real truth."

He climbed onto the bike. "Now let's go. Hopefully Priya cooked something good."

Varun hesitated, then nodded. The bike rolled forward, the forest closing behind them.

***

By the time they reached the house, the engine sputtered to a stop on the porch. Varun fumbled for the key.

"Hey, you two are back. I was waiting."

They turned. Priya stood at the gate, lunch box under her arm, dressed in a bright churidar. She glanced at the wilted plants with disapproval.

"Praba uncle would've been furious seeing this garden. He loved these plants."

"He liked gardening?" John asked.

"Yes. The best garden in the area. Now look at it." She shot a sharp glance at Varun. "This one doesn't bother."

Varun said nothing, disappearing inside.

John lingered. Priya stepped closer. "I know who you are. I saw the ad. I figured Varun would try to call you. But I didn't expect you to actually come."

"Then why play along with his lie?" John asked.

"Because he thinks everyone believes he's mad. Even me. But I never did. He's just... broken. If lying helps him feel like someone believes him, I don't mind."

John's smile was faint. "That's kind of you, Priya."

She opened the lunch box. "Rice, thoran, and—my special *Vana Sundari!*"

From inside: "I heard that!"

Priya laughed. "Good. He's not skipping lunch today."

John washed his hands and took a seat at the dining table.

"I was really hungry, Priya... And what is this *Vana Sundari*? I've never heard of it before."

"Chicken in a special green masala," she said. "Spicy, earthy—you'll love it."

Just then, Varun walked in, freshly washed, and joined them at the table.

Priya began serving food onto their plates.

"You know, you don't have to serve us. We can manage," Varun said, his tone a mix of politeness and mild protest.

"I know," Priya said cheerfully. "But I like feeding you, *Mallakuraja*."

"Don't call me that."

"Mallakuraja?" John asked.

"Monkey," Priya laughed. "He used to climb everything when we were kids."

"You two went to school together?" John asked, surprise.

"Yeah," Priya said, nodding. "Varun was two years ahead of me. Still acted like an old man even back then."

"Ohh... and Varun, you never mentioned any of your friends," John said between bites."Don't you have any?"

"I do," Varun replied, picking at his rice.

"But most of them are out of town now. Some moved abroad... chasing better opportunities."

"And you didn't?" John asked, glancing at him curiously.

Varun shook his head. "I didn't want to leave my dad alone here. That's why I started the newspaper delivery business. It let me stay close... be around if he needed anything."

John gave a thoughtful nod and continued eating.

"This dish of yours is really good, Priya. What was the name again?" John asked, savoring another bite.

"*Vana Sundari*," Priya replied with a proud smile, clearly pleased with the compliment.

"Well, *Vana Sundari* deserves a five-star review," John said, grinning as he reached for another bite.

Both of them finished eating and went to wash their hands. Priya quickly packed up the lunch box with practiced ease.

"Just leave it there, I'll clean it," Varun said, stepping toward her.

"No need," she replied with a quick smile. "I have to go now anyway. I'll bring something special for dinner. Bye!" She waved cheerfully and walked out the door, the lunch box tucked under her arm.

"She's a nice girl," John remarked.

Varun nodded quietly.

John stretched his arms and stifled a yawn.

"Let me get a bit of sleep. We can talk to your dad's friends this evening, right?"

"Yes, they'll be around the town area by then," Varun said.

"Good. Don't forget to wake me," John added, heading into the room.

"I won't," Varun said as John gently closed the door behind him.

John sat heavily on the bed, the soft creak of the frame the only sound in the quiet room. He reached for his bag and unzipped it carefully, removing the small handgun he had tucked discreetly into his waistband. For a moment, he turned it over in his hand, the weight of it a cold, familiar comfort. Then he placed it gently inside the bag and zipped it shut.

Stretching out on the bed, he let his head sink into the pillow. The day's images drifted through his mind, the strange calm of the forest, the eerie words of the old woman, the torn body at the crime scene. Everything felt tangled, incomplete, like a puzzle with a few key pieces still missing.

The sounds of the house faded as he slowly drifted into sleep.

CHAPTER 5

Vada and Tea

The sharp ring of his phone jolted John awake. He glanced at his watch—**3:30 p.m.** Already.

Rahul's name flashed on the screen. John sat up and answered.

"Good evening, Rahul."

A pause. "Yes... did you get anything on that?"

Another pause. "Oh, I see. Okay. Nothing serious. Thanks, Rahul. Bye."

He slipped the phone into his pocket and stepped into the hall.

"Varun?" he called.

Silence.

He crossed the hallway and knocked on Varun's door. Still nothing.

"Varun, you there?" John asked as he gently pushed the door open.

The room was a mess—clothes scattered on the floor, dust clinging to every surface. It felt abandoned, neglected. And there, in the middle of it all, Varun lay fast asleep, curled up like a child.

John shook him gently. "Varun. Get up."

Varun blinked, rubbing his eyes. "Oh... sorry, did I sleep too long?"

"No," John said. "But I just got a call from Rahul."

Varun sat up quickly. "The guy from the forest department, right? What did he say?"

"Freshen up first," John replied, already turning away. "We'll talk on the way. We need to meet your father's friends."

Varun frowned but nodded.

***

Back in his room, John changed into a clean shirt. He checked his gun, slid it into the holster at his back, and adjusted his clothes until it disappeared from view.

When he returned, Varun was waiting in the hall, eager for answers.

"He found records on last year's tiger attack," John said as they stepped outside. "The tiger was transferred to the Periyar Reserve. Old, turned man-eater. They kept it under observation for a month... then moved it to the Trivandrum Zoo."

Relief flickered across Varun's face. "So it wasn't a tiger."

"No," John agreed, climbing onto the bike. "Not that tiger. But we still can't rule out an animal entirely."

Varun's relief faded. He kicked the engine to life. "I'm telling you, sir—it wasn't an animal."

"Then let's find the truth," John said firmly. "First, your father's friends."

Varun nodded and eased the bike forward.

***

They left the forest road behind. The village opened before them, alive with evening bustle. Shops glowed under yellow bulbs. Children darted between parked bikes. The scent of fried snacks floated from a tea stall.

Varun stopped near two weathered motorcycles parked outside a small shop. "These are theirs," he said. "They should be inside."

John followed him in.

The tea shop was modest—plastic tables, metal chairs, glass shelves stacked with hot snacks glistening in oil. Behind the counter, a young man poured steaming tea into tumblers while an older cook tended a pan of bubbling vadas. Conversation and the clink of glasses filled the air.

"Varun!" a voice called from the back.

A lean man in his fifties waved, his grizzled beard breaking into a smile. Two others sat with him, shirts and lungis faded from years of wear.

Soman, Rajan, and Sasi—the old friends.

"Come, sit," Soman said, pulling a chair closer. Their eyes flicked to John, cautious but polite.

"This is John Uncle," Varun said. "Dad's old friend from Trivandrum."

John nodded politely. They shifted, posture turning respectful.

"Praba's friend," Rajan said warmly. "Please, sit. Have tea."

"Two teas," Rajan called to the counter. "And vada. The vada here's the best."

John smiled faintly. "Vada sounds good."

***

As they waited, Rajan asked, "So how long have you known Praba?"

John didn't blink. "We go way back. Met during his days in Chennai."

The lie rolled easily from his tongue. Varun glanced at him, surprised by how natural it sounded, but said nothing.

"I only recently learned what happened," John added, voice soft. "That's why I came."

The men exchanged glances, their faces clouding.

“It was unfortunate,” Sasi said at last.

“Yes,” Soman added. “We were with him that night. Drinking, laughing. We never thought it would be the last time.” His voice cracked with grief.

“Mmm... he was a good man,” John murmured with a sigh, the heaviness in his chest briefly escaping through the sound.

“When he called, he always talked about you guys... about the times you'd hang out in the forest,” John said, his voice casual yet tinged with genuine warmth. “He kept telling me to visit one day. Guess I was too late.”

Just then, the waiter arrived with their order, steaming vadas and cups of hot tea, the aroma briefly lifting the weight of the conversation.

“So,” John continued, breaking a piece of vada, “do you guys still hang out in the forest these days too?”

“No, we don’t,” Rajan said, shaking his head slowly. “It’s not the same without him. These days, this tea shop has become our usual spot. We haven't touched liquor in months."

"Oh... I see," John replied, nodding thoughtfully as he sipped his tea.

Rajan turned toward Varun, placing a warm hand on his shoulder. "And how are you these days, son?" he asked, giving him a gentle shake. "We know it hit you hard. It hit all of us. But you can't stay locked up at home forever. You need to talk to people, Varun."

His voice was soft, but full of genuine concern, like an elder who had seen enough loss to recognize the quiet damage it could do.

"I'm trying to, uncle," Varun said quietly, his voice barely above the hum of the tea shop.

John leaned forward slightly, changing the subject with casual precision. "So... did they catch the tiger?"

Rajan turned to him, the shift in topic pulling him from his concern. "No, they didn't," he said with a shrug. "The forest department claimed it must've wandered deep into the jungle."

***

"Ohh... okay," John said, sipping his tea.

Out of the corner of his eye, he noticed someone watching them. He didn't react immediately, just casually turned his head as he lifted the cup for another sip.

"One more vada, please," he told the waiter.

That brief turn gave him just enough time to scan the surroundings without drawing attention. Two men were seated directly across the shop. They had their eyes on him, but quickly looked away the moment he turned. Both wore shirts and lungis, their beards thick and unkempt, hair overgrown. Something about them didn't sit right with John. They looked like trouble.

He made a mental note of their faces, their posture, the way they gripped their tea glasses, too tight. Then, without showing any reaction, he turned back and continued the conversation with the group as if nothing had happened.

"You were right, the vada here is really good," John said to Rajan with a nod of appreciation.

Suddenly, he heard the scrape of plastic chairs behind him. The two men who had been watching him stood up. They walked to the counter and paid their bill. Nothing unusual on the surface, but John's eyes tracked them.

They headed out to a Royal Enfield Bullet parked nearby. Both climbed on, and without speaking a word, rode off.

John kept his expression neutral, but inside, his curiosity spiked. There was something off about them. Not just the way they stared earlier, but the way they moved. Too precise. Too controlled. Like men trained not to draw attention, but failing just enough to do the opposite.

He sipped his tea slowly, eyes narrowing.

He couldn't quite place it... but something about those two wasn't right.

"So, when did you come here?" Rajan's voice pulled John out of his thoughts.

"Just this morning," John replied, finishing the last sip of his tea. He glanced at Varun, who immediately caught the signal.

"Alright then, we'll get going," Varun said, standing up.

"Okay," Rajan nodded, his tone turning gentle. "Make sure you guys reach home before it gets too dark."

"Will do. Bye, guys," John said with a small wave to the group as he followed Varun out of the tea shop.

***

They walked side by side toward Varun's bike, the warm evening sun casting long shadows on the road behind them.

Outside, Varun started the bike. "We're going home?"

John climbed on behind him. "Not yet. First, the police station."

Varun glanced back, curiosity sharp. "Did you find something?"

John tapped his shoulder. "We'll talk later. Let's go."

The engine rumbled, carrying them down the road as the old friends watched from the tea shop doorway.

CHAPTER 6

Mysterious Duo

Varun's mind was racing.

Why did John suddenly want to visit the police station?

Had he found a clue?

He tried to keep calm, eyes fixed on the road as the bike rattled toward the Kallukad Police Station. Behind him, John sat silent, lost in his own thoughts.

The trio seemed harmless. They didn't look like people capable of murder, let alone staging it to look like a tiger attack.

But people can surprise you. They always do, John reminded himself.

***

The bike stopped in front of the station.

The building looked tired and weathered, its walls faded, its roof sagging. Only the bright blue and red board reading *Kallukad Police Station* gave it any presence. Inside the compound, seized bikes lay rusting, weeds sprouting from their frames. A dusty white Bolero jeep stood nearby, forgotten under a film of grime.

The air carried the low buzz of flies, the crackle of police radios, and the faint hum of the road outside.

John climbed off, adjusted his shirt, and checked his gun beneath it. He tapped Varun's shoulder. "Let's go."

But Varun didn't move. He sat staring at the ground, fingers drumming on the fuel tank.

John turned back. "What's wrong?"

"They don't like seeing me," Varun muttered.

"Why?"

"I've been here too many times... asking questions. They always pushed me out. They never wanted to help."

John nodded, weighing the pain in the young man's voice. "Alright. Stay here. I'll handle it."

He walked through the gate alone.

***

The station compound felt familiar—radios, murmurs, the shuffle of boots—echoes of his old life. He was halfway across the yard when a voice rang out.

"John sir! ... Is that really you?"

A tall, fit young policeman hurried out of the building and came closer, stopping to salute sharply..

John blinked in surprise. Even Varun, watching from the bike, looked startled.

"There's no need to salute a retired man," John said with a faint smile. "Mr...?"

"You don't remember me, sir? I was with you in Trivandrum."

Memory clicked into place. "Ah. Siddharth. Sorry, I must be getting old."

Siddharth grinned. "No, sir. You look exactly the same as you did at your retirement party." His voice softened with warmth. "What brings you to Kallukad, sir?"

Before John could reply, Siddharth spotted Varun outside. His smile vanished.

"How many times have I told you, Varun? Leave!" he barked.

"He's with me," John said firmly.

The words landed like a command. Siddharth froze, reminded who he was speaking to—his former superior.

He lowered his voice, eyes darting nervously. "Sir... don't tell me he's your client."

John just smiled. He didn't need to say more. Siddharth's face tightened with worry.

He glanced around, then leaned closer. "Sir... you should leave. This case is bigger than you think."

John's eyes narrowed. "And why is that?"

"I can't say. Not here. Please... come to my quarters. I'll explain."

John studied him for a beat, then gave a single nod.

***

Minutes later, Siddharth led them through winding lanes to a row of government quarters. He parked his bike outside a small single-bedroom house, looked around nervously, and unlocked the door.

"Stay here," John told Varun. The young man nodded reluctantly as John followed Siddharth inside.

The house was cramped, messy—half-empty glasses on the stand, a uniform shirt tossed over a chair. A bachelor's life.

"Sorry for the mess," Siddharth muttered, pulling up a chair.

John lowered himself into an armchair. "What is it, Siddharth? Don't hold back. I've been in the force too long—there's very little left that can surprise me."

Siddharth gave a nervous chuckle. "Well... hold on to that thought, sir. You will be surprised."

John leaned forward.

"Well... you didn't hear this from me, alright?" Siddharth said cautiously.

"Of course," John nodded. "Go on."

Siddharth leaned in, his voice low and steady.

Siddharth's voice dropped. "Sir, I've seen murders, suicides, accidents... but never anything like this. Varun's father—his limbs, his head... they weren't cut. They were *torn* from the body."

John's expression stilled, though his eyes sharpened. "Any bite marks? Claw wounds?"

Siddharth shook his head. "No. None. I was on night duty, one of the first at the scene. I saw the body with my own eyes."

John leaned back, the weight of it sinking in.

If true, Varun's story wasn't grief or shock. It was fact.

"What about the claw marks? The ones on the body later?" John asked.

Siddharth exhaled, gaze dropping. "That's what I need to tell you. At first, there weren't any. But on the next day, everything changed. Two men came to the station. Not locals. Military type. No uniforms, but clean haircuts, soldier posture, guns under their shirts. They went straight to the S.I.'s office."

John's jaw tightened.

"They collected our phones. Took every file, every photo, every log connected to the case. Even the forensics evidence. Then they went to the morgue. By the time the body was returned, those claw marks had been carved in."

John closed his eyes briefly. "That explains it."

"Yes, sir. The S.I. told us to forget everything. Said it was above our pay grade."

Siddharth's frustration cracked through. "But why? Why would the military—or whoever they were—intervene in a forest killing?"

"He saw something," John murmured. "Something he wasn't meant to."

Siddharth leaned closer. "Please, sir. Don't tell Varun. If he finds out, we're all in danger."

John gave him a steady look. "Don't worry. I'll handle it."

"Did they use a bike?"

"Yes, a Royal Enfield Bullet. Wait, how did you"

"Just a hunch," John muttered, leaning back.

"Okay... is there anything else?"

"No sir, that's all I know"

"Ok, then I will leave, call me if you have anything else to say"

"I don't have your number anymore sir, it was on my old phone."

John scribbled his number on a slip from his notepad and handed it to Siddharth. Then he turned and stepped out of the house.

***

Outside, dusk had deepened into night. Varun straightened on the bike as John approached. "So? What happened?"

"Later. At home," John said.

It was 7:30 p.m. when they rode back through the forest, the trees whispering in the dark. John's gaze lingered on the place where Praba had fallen. The poor man saw something he shouldn't have... and someone made sure he never spoke.

***

By the time they reached the house, the forest had settled into its eerie night calm.

John climbed down and waited while Varun parked the bike. A soft yellow light from the electric pole illuminated the front yard.

"So? What did he say?" Varun asked, eyes wide with anticipation.

"First open the door," John replied. "We'll talk inside."

Varun walked up to the door, then stopped abruptly. "The door's open, I locked it before" he said, confused.

John moved forward quickly. The door was open.

Without hesitation, John drew his gun.

Varun froze at the sight of it. He hadn't known John was carrying.

John flipped the switch on the porch. Nothing. The lights didn't turn on.

From the corner of his eye, he noticed lights in the neighbors' houses. Power wasn't the problem.

John pulled a small torch from his pocket and moved in with his weapon raised. Varun stayed close behind..

The living room was untouched. So was John's room.

He crept toward Varun's room. The door was closed. He nudged it open.

Unmoved. Everything was where it had been.

"Where's the main switch?" John asked.

"Outside," Varun replied.

They stepped back into the yard. Varun pointed to the gray metal box on the side wall. John opened it with his torch.

The main switch had been turned off manually.

John flipped it back up. The porch lights flickered on.

He exhaled quietly.

They returned inside. Varun saw and picked up the lunch box Priya had left on the porch.

Inside, John sat down at the dining table, his gun in front of him. His eyes were closed, deep in thought.

Varun placed the lunch box down and took the seat across from him.

"Sir... what just happened? Did someone rob my house?"

John stirred, his eyelids heavy as he forced them open. His voice came out low and strained.

"No, Varun. They weren't here for your house. They were looking for me."

Varun blinked, his confusion sharpening into disbelief.

"You? Why would anyone come after you?"

John sat up slowly, his expression unreadable.

"They saw us at the tea shop. They wanted to know more."

"You mean Rajan uncle and the others?"

John shook his head.

"No. Two men. Strangers. They were watching from the corner table."

Varun's voice cracked. "Who were they? Do they have something to do with my father's death?"

John hesitated, then gave a single, heavy nod. "Yes."

Varun's face lit with anger and desperate hope. "Then if we catch them, we'll finally know what happened!"

John sighed. "It's not that simple."

"Why not?" Varun pressed.

"There are... far more complicated forces at play here," John said, his tone grave.

Varun clenched his fists.

"What complications? Just tell me the truth. Did that police officer say something to you?"

John met his eyes.

"Yes. He did. And that's why I'm telling you, this isn't straightforward. You need to calm down and listen to me. Do you understand?"

Varun drew in a sharp breath, forcing himself to steady his voice.

"Okay," he said at last, quieter this time.

John leaned forward, his tone firm.

"And you have to promise me... this information stays between us."

Varun frowned.

"But why?"

"Because," John replied, his eyes narrowing, "that's what's best for both of us."

Varun hesitated, then nodded.

"Fine. I won't tell anyone."

John gave a dry chuckle, though there was no humor in it.

"Even if you did, no one would believe you."

Varun's gaze sharpened, searching John's face for answers.

"What do you mean?"

John's voice dropped, heavy with reluctance.

"Your father's death... it's connected to the army."

Varun froze. His lips parted, but for a moment, no sound came out. Finally, he managed a whisper.

"The army? How... how could that be?"

John shook his head slowly, frustration flickering across his features.

"That, I can't say for certain. Maybe your father saw something he shouldn't have. Maybe he stumbled into something much bigger than himself. But one thing is certain, he witnessed something that night that cost him his life."

Varun leaned forward, his voice sharp.

"How do you know the army is involved?"

John's eyes darkened as he recalled the conversation.

"Siddharth, the police officer I met, was once a subordinate of mine. He told me something disturbing. Two men had come to the station after your father's case was filed. They took away every scrap of evidence, even the officers' phones. Everything connected to the investigation was wiped clean."

Varun's breath hitched. John continued, his tone heavy.

"And Siddharth said something else... When he first saw your father's body, there were no claw marks. Just like you insisted. The marks were added later."

Varun's eyes widened. He shot up from his chair, his voice trembling with rage.

"Yes... Yes! I told you, didn't I? I told you there were no claw marks! You didn't believe me!" His fists clenched. "So those men... they carved those marks onto my father's body?"

John lowered his head, regret etched across his face.

"Yes, Varun. It seems so. And I'm sorry... sorry for doubting you."

Varun sat down on the chair

Varun collapsed back into the chair, his anger giving way to exhaustion.

"It's okay, sir. I just... I just want the truth." He looked at John, eyes burning with determination.

"What do we do now? We can't stop here. We need to know what really happened."

John's voice was low, carrying the weight of caution.

"Well, Varun... it won't be as easy as you think. These aren't just thugs or petty criminals. They're the army. They raided this house simply because they saw me with you today. That alone should tell you how far their reach extends."

Varun swallowed hard, the realization sinking in.

"You mean... they could be watching us even now?"

John's expression grew grim.

“Exactly. From what I can tell, they’re not the official army, maybe a covert unit running secret operations here in Kallukadu. And they don’t want anyone looking too closely.”

He paused, letting the silence weigh heavy between them.

“And if we keep snooping around, Varun... we might find ourselves in far more trouble than we can handle.”

Varun’s voice cracked with disbelief.

“So... we just leave this? Pretend nothing happened and never talk about it again? Is that what you’re telling me?”

John leaned back, his gaze heavy, the lines on his face deepening with weariness.

“Well... that would be the wise choice, Varun. I know it’s a bitter pill to swallow, but sometimes walking away is the only way to survive.”

He studied the young man’s eyes, the storm brewing within them. A faint, almost resigned smile touched his lips.

"But my gut tells me you're not the type to let this go... are you?"

Varun shot up from his chair, his chest heaving as the words tumbled out, raw and unfiltered.

"I don't care who they are, sir! I want to know what happened to my father. He was a good man... My father never harmed anyone. And yet..." His voice cracked, anger and grief colliding. "He was lying there, on the forest floor, torn apart... limb by limb. Like an animal. I need to know why. Why would someone do that to him?"

The room fell silent under Varun's grief and rage. John exhaled, knowing the fire in him wouldn't be smothered by warnings.

John's gaze softened, though his voice carried the weight of warning.

"I understand your pain, Varun. But the hunt for the truth... it can be deadly for both of us. Still" he paused, his words deliberate, "I'll stand with you till the end. We'll find the truth. Tomorrow we begin. For now, get some rest."

Varun's eyes shimmered with long-lost hope. He nodded at John with quiet admiration before turning away, his footsteps fading into the silence of the house.

John sat at the dining table, hands clasped, mind weighed down by the day's ordeals. He rubbed his temples, knowing sleep would not come easily.

Unseen by either of them, a monitor flickered in a dimly lit room far away. On its grainy screen, John sat hunched at the dining table while Varun disappeared into the hallway.

A man leaned forward, his eyes narrowing at the feed. He pressed a finger to his comms, his voice low but urgent.

"Sir... we have a problem."

CHAPTER 7

Old Forest God

The shrill buzz of the alarm stirred John from sleep. He reached for the phone, silencing it with a weary swipe.

5:00 a.m. glowed on the screen.

Rain hammered the roof, a steady roar filling the silence of the house. John rose, the floor cool beneath his feet, and stepped into the hallway. Varun's faint snores drifted from behind his door.

John opened the main door, dragged a chair closer to the doorway and lowered himself onto it. The rain poured in sheets beyond the porch, the world outside blurred by water and mist. He sat still, listening to its rhythm, but his mind refused to quiet.

Was this the right choice, entangling himself in Varun's grief, knowing full well it would lead to danger? He should have steered the boy away, spoken harder truths, and left this place behind. That would have been the wise thing.

But the mystery lingered like a thorn under his skin. What really happened that night? The questions clawed at him, refusing to let go.

And there was Varun. Even if John walked away, the boy would chase the answers alone, blind, reckless, and far too young for the darkness he was stepping into.

John leaned back, eyes fixed on the curtain of rain. No, he thought. If trouble was coming, better the boy had someone to stand beside him.

***

Through the curtain of rain, John noticed a figure moving along the dirt path. A large umbrella tilted low, shielding the face. The figure stopped in front of the house, peering at him through the downpour, and raised a hand in greeting.

John squinted, uncertain, the rain distorting the silhouette. Then the figure began to approach, each step deliberate on the muddy ground. As she drew nearer, recognition struck him.

It was Priya.

She smiled warmly, a small light against the gray morning. Dressed in a shirt and trousers, she carried a large steel container in her hands, its weight obvious by the way she steadied it against her hip.

"Good morning. You're up early," Priya said as she came closer, rain dripping from her umbrella.

"Good morning," John replied with a faint smile. "Old habits. Where did you head off to this early?"

"I went to the milkman's house to collect today's milk."

"Oh? You carry that every day?" His eyes flicked to the heavy steel container in her hands.

"Usually I take the scooter," she said, adjusting her grip. "But with this rain, I thought I'd walk."

"I see." John nodded. "Varun mentioned you're a businesswoman."

Priya chuckled softly. "Ah, not that big. But yes, I get regular orders."

"That's good to hear."

She glanced toward the house. "Has Varun woken up yet?"

"No, still asleep."

"Alright then, I should be going." She turned, taking a few steps before pausing.

Without looking back, she asked quietly, "Did you find the killer?"

John's gaze hardened. "Not yet," he said. "But we will."

Priya hesitated, then turned back toward John. The rain drummed steadily on her umbrella as she stepped closer to the porch.

"I have something to tell you," she said softly.

John straightened in his chair, his eyes narrowing. "What is it?"

She glanced at him, uncertainty flickering across her face. “I don’t think you’ll believe me.”

John leaned forward, his tone firm. “Try me. I’ve heard more than my share of unbelievable things in the past few days.”

Priya’s voice was barely above the sound of the rain.

“I saw something that night.” She held John’s gaze, her eyes trembling with the weight of the memory.

John narrowed his eyes. “Which night?” he asked, rising slowly to his feet.

“The night Praba uncle died,” Priya whispered, her eyes falling to the ground as if the words themselves were too heavy to carry.

John’s posture stiffened. “What did you see?”

“I... I don’t know,” she stammered, her breath quickening. “But it wasn’t human.”

John’s face sharpened, his jaw tightening. The storm seemed to grow louder around them.

“Not human...?” he repeated, his voice low, testing the weight of her words.

"Yes." Her voice cracked. "I was terrified. I didn't tell Varun... he was already breaking apart. Everyone called him crazy. I couldn't make it worse."

John took a slow step closer, the rain sliding down his face like cold glass.

"Priya," he said, steady and measured, "just tell me what you saw."

"That night... I was riding back from a late cake delivery," Priya began, her voice trembling. "I came through the forest path, it was past late night. Then I heard it... a deafening sound, followed by a scream, inhuman, unholy."

She gripped her arms, as if holding herself together. "I froze. And then, something leapt across the road, right in front of my scooter. The headlight caught it for a second. It vanished into the trees before I could even breathe. I still don't know what I saw... but it wasn't human."

"Not... human?" John's voice was low, steady as stone.

Priya's throat worked around the answer, her gaze sinking toward the dirt. "Yes. An animal... but not one I've ever seen."

John's eyes narrowed, the silence between them taut, broken only by the faint drip of water from the eaves. "And the sound you heard, was it a gunshot?"

"I think so," she whispered. Her voice quivered, thin as glass. "I'm not certain. It was loud, too loud."

"From which side did you hear it? Left or Right?"

"Left...it was from the left side"

John sat, piecing threads in his head.

"Did you tell anyone else?"

Priya shook her head. "No. They wouldn't believe me."

"And you think this ties to Varun's father's death?"

"Yes."

"Then why not tell Varun?"

Her eyes clouded. "He was spiraling after Praba uncle's death. Everyone already thinks he's losing it. If I added talk of a... forest monster, they'd call him mad for sure. The tiger story was easier. I thought you" she hesitated, "you might be the right person to hear this. Maybe help him."

"Alright," John said, leaning forward. "Do you remember when exactly this happened?"

Priya frowned, eyes searching the ground. "I... I don't know. Maybe sometime after eight-thirty, I think."

John nodded slowly. "And the place?"

"Mmm..." He hesitated, as if replaying the memory in his head. "Near the turn that leads into the deep forest."

John's mind worked quickly, trying to piece the fragments together. A vague time after eight-thirty. A gunshot, maybe. And now, a location, near the turn into the deep forest. None of it was solid, but every shard of detail mattered. He could almost feel the picture forming, faint outlines waiting to be filled in.

"I have to go"

John's thoughts scattered at the sound of Priya's words.

"Alright... is there anything else you remember?" he asked.

"No. After that happened, I rushed home. The next morning, I heard about Praba uncle's death."

"Okay. Call me if anything else comes back. Did you notice anything suspicious around the house last night?"

Priya frowned. "No... I didn't. Why do you ask?"

John shook his head lightly. "Nothing. Just asking."

"Hmm. Alright then... goodbye."

She pulled her umbrella tighter and walked away into the rain, her figure dissolving into the gray curtain of water.

***

John sat on the chair, watching the rain pour outside, his mind piecing together the new revelations.

"Things are only getting more tangled with time," John muttered under his breath. He pulled out his phone, the cold glow of the screen brightening this face. 5:30 a.m. stared back at him.

John rose and crossed to Varun's room, tapping on the door. No answer. The rain outside had softened to a distant murmur..

"Varun... Varun, wake up," John called.

The bed creaked within. "Coming," came the groggy reply.

John returned to the dining table, waiting. Moments later, Varun stepped out, rubbing sleep from his eyes.

"What happened, sir? Why are you up so early?"

"It's not early. It's already five-thirty. Sit, I need to talk to you."

Varun splashed water on his face and joined him. "What is it?"

"We have new information."

Varun frowned. "What information?"

"The night your father died... Priya saw something in the forest."

"Priya? Why didn't she tell me?"

"She thought she was protecting you. And she isn't sure what she saw."

Varun leaned forward, tense. "What did she see?"

"She heard a gunshot. Then... something crossed her path. An animal, but not one she could recognize."

"What kind of animal?"

"That we don't know. But the timing and place line up with your father's death. She saw it after eight-thirty, your father was killed around nine."

"Where exactly?"

"Near the turn into the deep forest."

Varun shook his head, anger flickering in his eyes. "So it was just an animal? No, sir. That's the same dead end. How could an animal tear a man apart like that?"

John leaned back in his chair, his expression thoughtful.

"We don't know what it was," he said slowly. "She isn't sure what she saw. But she is certain about one thing, it wasn't human. It was... something she couldn't explain."

"Like a monster?" Varun asked, his voice uneasy.

John sighed. "If you're riding through the night, with nothing but a scooter's headlight to guide you, even a shadow can look like a monster. I can't say for sure what she saw."

"Then what do we do?"

"We go there ourselves. Take a look. Maybe we'll find something."

Varun straightened. "So... we go now?"

"Yes. Get ready. We're leaving soon."

"Okay," Varun muttered, slipping into his room.

John washed his face, the cold water waking him up fully. He entered his room, dressed quickly, and slid his pistol into a holster tucked behind his back. Gathering his notes and wallet, he stepped out. Varun was already waiting, ready and alert.

"Let's go," John said as he pushed open the door.

***

Soon, both men stepped into the damp dawn. Varun wheeled out his bike. John holstered his pistol beneath his shirt and swung onto the pillion seat.

The bike coughed to life and rolled forward, tires spitting mud. The forest pressed close, rain whispering against their clothes.

After a while, Varun asked, “What do you think really happened, sir?”

John’s eyes scanned the blur of trees. “There’s something in this forest. Your father... was in the wrong place at the wrong time.”

“I’ve lived here my whole life,” Varun said. “Never seen anything strange. Except... children’s stories.”

“Stories?” John asked.

“They say there’s a forest god here. One who kills anyone who harms the woods.”

John chuckled. “A violent god.”

Varun nodded. “They said long ago, some men went to cut trees. Found dead. People said the forest god killed them.”

"Interesting," John murmured. "How long ago did this happen?"

"I don't know. I only heard about it back when I was in school."

John smiled faintly. "Children do have a talent for imagination."

"Maybe. But when you connect it now..."

"Are you saying a god killed your father?" John's smile was wry. "I'd say a tiger makes a better suspect."

"Sometimes one man's god is another man's demon," he added softly.

***

The bike slowed to a halt near the turnoff, its tires sinking slightly into the rain-soaked road. The downpour had softened to a drizzle, mist clinging to the trees. John swung off the bike and stepped onto the mud, his shoes sinking with each step as he studied the path vanishing into the forest's shadows.

"So, she saw it here," John murmured, half to himself. "Coming back from town... and the sound came from that way." He gestured toward the path leading deeper into the woods.

Varun cut the engine.

"Any houses down that path?" John asked.

"No. Just forest."

John crouched, running his hand along a set of grooves pressed into the wet earth. "Take a look."

Varun leaned closer. His eyes widened. "Tire tracks."

"Not just tires," John said, his voice low. "Truck tracks. Heavy ones."

Varun frowned. "But this road leads nowhere. Why would a truck head into the deep forest?"

John's gaze followed the tracks into the trees. "Then why is a truck here?"

***

Varun rolled the bike forward. John swung back onto the seat, and together they rode into the waiting shadows of the forest, the muddy path swallowing them whole.

"Have you ever been this deep into the forest?" John asked.

"Yeah, many years ago. I sometimes went with some friends," Varun replied.

"Is there anything worth seeing inside?"

"Not much, just monkeys, elephants, wild boar... oh, and a small waterfall."

"Ohh... do the animals ever cause trouble?"

"No," Varun said with a laugh.

"Animals don't bother people much. It's usually people who bother them."

"Yeah... true," John agreed with a faint smile.

As they ventured deeper, the forest thickened into shadow. The rising sun struggled against the dense canopy above, its light swallowed by layers of interwoven leaves, leaving the path ahead dim and hushed.

They crossed a small waterfall spilling across the path, its flow stronger. Varun guided the bike carefully through the rushing water, wheels slipping slightly before finding grip. On the other side, the muddy trail still bore the deep grooves of truck tires, etched clearly into the earth. They kept close to the tracks, following them deeper into the forest.

"The path is nearing its end, sir," Varun said.

"Alright," John replied.

As the trail curved ahead, the forest opened just enough to reveal a black truck parked at the edge of the path.

Varun eased the bike to a halt, his gaze fixed on the vehicle. He glanced back at John, who was already staring intently at the truck, his eyes sharp with suspicion.

Without a word, John swung off the bike. His hand slid to his holster, drawing his gun as he advanced cautiously.

Varun rolled the bike to the side of the trail and hurried after him. John raised a hand, signaling for silence, before stepping closer. The driver's seat was empty. The truck's cargo hold was sealed under a sheet of dull metal.

John inspected the rear. The loading bay door wasn't locked. He gestured for Varun to stay back. Taking position, John aimed his weapon, then gripped the handle and pulled the door open in one swift motion, the barrel of his gun steady as he aimed into the darkness inside.

The truck's cargo bay was empty except for stacks of boxes. John motioned to Varun, who climbed in and pried one open.

"These are... food items," Varun said, pulling out a sack of vegetables.

"Food?" John echoed, frowning. "Out here?"

Varun nodded. "Yeah. Kitchen supplies. Rice, oil... nothing strange."

John's gaze drifted past the truck, to where the muddy road ended. A narrow trail cut deeper into the forest, almost hidden, its damp soil marked with fresh footprints. He signaled Varun down.

"They went this way," John muttered.

"Then let's follow," Varun said, already stepping forward.

John caught his arm. "Stop."

Varun blinked at him. "What is it?"

John's eyes searched his. "Do you really want to move forward, Varun?"

"Yes," Varun said firmly. "I want to know the truth."

"This will be risky. I don't think we should."

"If you're afraid, you can stay here, sir. But I'm going. I want answers."

John gave a humorless smile. "It's not fear. It's logical. Look at what they're hauling" he nodded toward the truck

"A truck in the deep forest, fresh supplies, no villages nearby... This isn't poachers, Varun. Someone's stationed out here. And that means government or military."

Varun straightened his shoulders. "So, you want me to turn back?"

"I know you won't." John's hand tightened around his pistol. "Fine. But stay close to me, and do exactly as I say. Understood?"

Varun nodded. "Understood."

***

John stepped onto the trail, weapon raised, eyes flicking over every shadow. Varun followed at his heel. The footprints were clear, pressed deep into the wet soil. As they moved forward, the ground sloped upward, the forest thickening, branches interlaced above them like a ceiling that shut out the light.

"What do you think they're doing here?" Varun whispered.

"Experimenting. Researching. Something they don't want seen."

They moved cautiously forward, the ground rising beneath their feet as the terrain grew more uneven. The forest thickened around them, its shadows pressing closer. In the distance, the shrill cries of monkeys echoed, mingling with the flutter of unseen birds, adding an eerie undertone to the silence between them.

Suddenly, John heard a sharp sound behind him. He spun around to see Varun collapsed on the ground.

"Varun... Varun!" John called out, but there was no response.

His eyes widened when he spotted a dart jutting from Varun's shoulder. As John rushed forward, another dart whistled through the air and struck his own shoulder. With a grunt, he yanked it out, staring at the tiny needle in disbelief.

He whipped his head around, scanning the dense forest for the attacker, but it was too late, the burning numbness spread through his arm, his legs grew heavy, and as his body betrayed him under the drug's grip, John's vision blurred before darkness swallowed him whole.

CHAPTER 8

Secrets

"Sir... wake up."

Varun's urgent whisper cut through the haze. He nudged John's shoulder until the older man's eyes fluttered open.

Blinking hard, John scanned his surroundings. Varun sat beside him, his arms twisted awkwardly behind his back. Instinctively, John tried to move—his wrists burned. They were bound tight with zip ties. His legs too.

"Thank God," Varun muttered. "You've been out for a while."

John shifted, attempting to rise, but the effort was useless. His legs were strapped to the chair with the same plastic restraints as Varun's.

He finally took in the room. A cold, metallic table stood in front of them, with another empty chair on the other side. A camera in the corner blinked red, recording their every move. The walls were bare except for a heavy metal door and a large mirror dominating one side. Above them, a single LED tube light, casting a harsh white glow that made the room feel even colder.

"Where are we, sir?" Varun asked, his voice unsteady.

"We're in an interrogation room," John replied flatly.

"Interrogation room?"

"Look at the glass," John said, nodding toward the mirror. "It's two-way."

"Two-way?" Varun asked, his voice trembling.

"There's someone on the other side watching us," John replied calmly.

Varun's eyes darted to the mirror, panic creeping in. "Let us go... we're not criminals!" he shouted.

"Be quiet, Varun," John said in a steady tone.

Varun turned to him, confused. "How can you be this calm? They might kill us!"

"If they wanted us dead, it would've happened already," John reasoned, his eyes fixed on the mirror. "They want something else. My guess is... they'll talk. Until then, we wait."

"I've been awake for at least an hour, sir. No one came," Varun muttered, his voice shaky.

"Believe me, they will," John replied firmly. "I've been on the other side of this table more times than I can count. This is a tactic, they're trying to wear us down before the questioning starts. They've got all the time in the world, Varun. So be patient. Don't spiral. I know this is scary... just breathe. In and out."

Varun swallowed hard and did as told, forcing himself to inhale deeply and exhale, again and again, trying to keep his panic at bay.

***

Suddenly, a loud metallic clang echoed from the door. Someone was unlocking it. Both John and Varun snapped their eyes toward it, tense as hounds on alert.

The heavy door creaked open, and two figures stepped inside.

The first was a brute of a man, broad shoulders filling the doorway, a black t-shirt stretched across his chest, camo pants tucked into combat boots. His head was shaved clean, but a thick beard framed his face, giving him the look of a hardened soldier. Everything about him screamed: highly trained, dangerous.

Beside him walked a stark contrast, a man in a pristine white lab coat, clutching a folder of files in one hand. His gray hair was slicked back with oil, his smile disturbingly pleased, as though he'd been waiting for this moment.

The man in the lab coat pulled out the chair opposite them and sat down with deliberate calm. He placed the files on the table, one by one, as if savoring the silence in the room. His fingers tapped the covers before he spoke, his voice smooth and measured.

"John Thomas..." he said, letting the name hang in the air.

"Varun Prabakaran..." he continued, his smile widening slightly.

Then his tone shifted, softer, barely above a whisper: "Prabakaran Rameshan."

Beside him, the soldier stood like a sentinel, broad, immovable, his eyes fixed on John and Varun as though waiting for the slightest wrong move.

The man in the lab coat rested his hands on the table, his faint smile never leaving.

"Before we begin... A-7, cut them loose. It looks uncomfortable."

The soldier moved instantly, pulling a knife from his belt. He stepped behind John and Varun, slicing through the plastic restraints with precise, practiced motions.

As he leaned in, John caught a glimpse of the man's forearm, a black demon tattoo, its horns curling up his veins as though they were part of the ink.

John brought his hands forward quickly, flexing his fingers as the blood rushed back, a dull numbness prickling through them.

"Don't worry," the man in the lab coat said lightly, watching John's discomfort with amusement. "The feeling will pass in a few hours."

He leaned back in his chair, eyes glinting behind the smile. "Hello, John. Hello, Varun. Allow me to introduce myself... You may call me Director. I've been hearing quite a lot about you two."

***

The Director slid John's file across the table, noticeably thicker than the others. He opened it with deliberate care, flipping through the pages as though savoring each detail.

"You've had quite the career, Mr. John," he began, his tone calm but probing. "Wife... passed away from cancer, four years ago. My condolences." His eyes flicked up briefly, then back to the file.

He turned a page, scanning quickly. "Ah... the Reaper Chandran case. That was one of yours, wasn't it? A difficult man to bring down.

Yet, you did." The Director's smile widened faintly. "Your reputation precedes you."

"Your daughter, working in the UK as a nurse. Married to Mr. James, a UK citizen. One child." The Director's smile curved slightly. "So... you're a grandfather."

He leaned forward, his tone turning sharper. "But the things you've been doing, Mr. John... not exactly grandfatherly, are they?"

John didn't respond, his face unreadable, eyes fixed on the Director.

Varun, meanwhile, sat in stunned silence. He had spent the past few days alongside John, yet so much of the man's life was a mystery to him. Hearing about John's past, his family, even the legendary cases he had worked on, it was like discovering he'd been walking beside a stranger all along.

***

"Next, we have Mr. Varun," the Director said, lifting the second file from the stack. He opened it slowly, his eyes scanning the first page.

"Varun... son of Prabakaran..." He paused deliberately, then looked up at the young man. "It was truly unfortunate, what happened to your father, Mr. Varun."

Varun's face flushed red with anger. "Why did you kill him?" he snapped, rising to his feet.

The soldier A7 didn't move a muscle. His voice alone carried the weight of command. "Sit. Down."

The calm authority in his tone struck harder than a shout. Varun froze under the man's gaze, his anger faltering. Slowly, he sank back into the chair, his fists clenched tight.

John said nothing. His eyes never left the Director, studying him carefully.

"I know how you feel, Mr. Varun," the Director said, his voice flat. "But your father's death was an accident. Wrong place, wrong time. We had nothing to do with it."

John leaned forward, eyes locked. "That's why you dressed it up as a tiger attack?"

The Director's lips curved into a thin smile.

"You are sharp, Mr. John. You've been the talk of this place for the last two days." He slid Varun's file back across the table, never breaking eye contact.

"Yes. We altered the report. It was necessary. Some truths are better buried."

"I want to know the truth... What really happened to my father?" Varun demanded.

The director leaned back, his voice calm but edged with menace. "Let's say I tell you the truth, then what? You'll run around telling everyone else, isn't it?"

"I give you my word," John cut in firmly. "We won't breathe a word of it. This boy deserves to know the truth."

The director gave a dry chuckle. "Promises hold no value here, Mr. John. You know you're not in a position to bargain. I can make sure neither of you walks out of this place."

Varun's face drained of color, fear gripping him. But John's expression remained calm, almost amused.

"You could kill us both and call it another tiger attack," John said evenly, a faint smile tugging at his lips. "But would it really be that easy? I'm certain you already had a hard time covering up your last mistake. You wouldn't want to go through that mess again. And besides... if you meant to kill us, you'd have done it back in the forest. Why bring us here for a friendly chat?"

The director leaned back in his chair, studying John in silence. After a moment, he leaned forward again, a faint smile tugging at his lips.

"You're sharp, Mr. John... so let's not waste time. I don't want you or this boy sniffing around my operations or whispering about them to anyone."

John's eyes didn't waver. "That can be arranged. But in return, we want the truth. Tell us what really happened that night."

The director let out a long breath, steadying himself, before rising to his feet. He gathered the files with deliberate care, his expression unreadable, and moved toward the cold, metal door. Just as his hand touched the handle, he stopped and slowly turned his head back. His gaze lingered on John and Varun, sharp and heavy.

"Come..."

***

The single word cut through the silence like a command.

John and Varun stood, exchanging a wary glance before following. Behind them, the soldier moved into step, his boots striking the floor with a dull, rhythmic thud, each one echoing like a warning as the group left the room.

As they stepped out of the room, John's eyes adjusted to the stark brightness around him. The place looked like a laboratory, white floors polished to a sterile shine, cold LED lights humming faintly overhead. They passed through a heavy gate, the director sliding his card to unlock it. The metallic click echoed sharply, making John's instincts tighten.

Inside, the room was alive. Men and women in lab coats moved briskly between workstations, speaking in hushed tones, tapping on keyboards, scribbling notes. But it wasn't the scientists that caught John's attention, it was the soldiers.

They stood in the corners like shadows given flesh. Tall, broad, and disciplined, their sheer size was unnatural, their muscles straining against their uniforms. Most wore thick beards, their identical attire a mirror of the soldier trailing behind John and Varun. Their presence wasn't just for protection, it was intimidation, a silent reminder of power.

John felt Varun tense beside him. He didn't blame him. Something about this place whispered danger in every polished surface and every guarded glance.

As they walked, John's eyes caught a table scattered with strange diagrams. The sketches showed an animal, alien in form, nothing he had ever seen before. He studied it for a second, but the shapes were too unfamiliar for him to make sense of.

They reached another reinforced door. The Director swiped his card and pressed his thumb against a scanner before it unlocked. Inside, the room was lined with racks of heavy, bright-orange protective hazmat suits. The Director began putting one on.

"Wear it," he instructed.

John and Varun hesitated, but the soldier behind them helped secure the bulky gear. The suit felt cumbersome at first, yet it carried the weight and solidity of armor.

The Director moved to a control panel and pressed a button. With a hiss, the next door slid open. He stepped inside, and John, Varun, and the soldier followed. As soon as they crossed the threshold, the door behind them sealed shut.

Varun's face tightened. He looked at John, uneasy.

"Don't worry," John whispered. "It's just a sterilizing process."

A second later, jets hidden in the walls activated. A sudden blast of liquid sprayed from every direction, drenching them in a fine, chemical mist.

After that, the next door slid open and they stepped inside. This room was busier, people in hazmat suits moved about, some focused on glowing screens, others clutching pump-action shotguns. In the very center stood a massive glass chamber, sealed tight. Inside it, more hazmat-clad figures walked slowly, their movements deliberate, as though conducting tests.

One of them broke away and approached the director, handing him a tablet.

"Sir, the results you requested," the person said through the muffled suit.

"Thank you," the director replied, his eyes already fixed on the screen as he began walking toward the glass chamber.

John trailed behind, scanning the room, when Varun's uneasy voice cut through the low hum of machinery.

"Sir... what is that?"

They were only a few feet from the glass chamber now. John followed Varun's trembling hand, pointing toward something inside. His eyes widened, and his steps faltered. For a moment he was struck dumb, his jaw dropped as he stared at the sight within.

John's eyes followed Varun's trembling finger, landing on the figure inside the glass chamber. At first, he thought it was a corpse. A human, maybe. But as his gaze adjusted as he walked near the glass, his breath caught in his throat.

It wasn't human. Not entirely.

Inside the chamber, bathed in a soft light that mimicked warm sunlight, lay the creature. At first glance, its form was unmistakably humanoid, but unlike any human John or Varun had ever seen. Its body seemed woven from living wood, its skin a tapestry of twisting vines and hardened bark, as though a forest had chosen to take shape in flesh.

Its chest rose and fell in slow, measured breaths, though the figure remained utterly still, locked in some deep, unnatural slumber. Closed eyelids hid whatever secrets its gaze might hold, but delicate green veins pulsed faintly beneath, glowing like fireflies trapped beneath its skin.

What unsettled John most wasn't the monstrous detail, but the strange, impossible beauty of it. The lines of its body carried an elegance, like the careful design of nature itself. Flowers bloomed faintly along its shoulders, their petals frozen mid-blossom. Its hair looked like threads of moss interwoven with silver strands, flowing over the table like a river of forest twilight.

Even in its slumber, the creature radiated a quiet, unsettling power, a warning wrapped in beauty.

John's jaw tightened, a cold chill crawling down his spine.

Varun whispered, almost to himself, "It's... alive," as he drifted closer to the glass, eyes wide with disbelief.

The Director, amused by their reactions, stepped forward, positioning himself between them.

"This," he said, voice carrying a strange mix of pride and dread, "is Project Vrikshara. What you see before you isn't human. It's something far older... something ancient."

He raised a hand, hovering just above the glass, careful not to touch it.

"Its body mirrors the forest itself, bark for skin, veins that run with moss, bones like roots twisted. Some of my men call it a forest god... others whisper it's a curse. What we do know is simple, it is old. Very old."

The Director's gaze shifted back to John and Varun, his eyes narrowing, sharp as blades.

"It sleeps now, dormant, hibernating, healing itself."

With that, he turned and began walking toward the reinforced door of the glass chamber. John and Varun hesitated, then followed in silence, the soldier's heavy steps trailing close behind.

Inside the chamber, the director raised a hand, signaling the other hazmat-suited personnel to leave. They obeyed without a word, slipping out through the sealed door. The soldier remained outside, posted like a silent sentinel, eyes locked on the group.

John and Varun's gaze was fixed on the creature lying at the center of the room. Drawn forward, they stepped closer, their footsteps echoing faintly on the sterile floor. The Director lingered near its head, his posture calm but his eyes watchful.

"We first discovered its existence in 1988," the Director began, his voice low, almost reverent. "Since then, we've done nothing but observe. It rarely shows aggression. In fact..." he paused, studying the creature's bark-like chest rising faintly with dormant breath, "it is shy.

Passive by nature. It doesn't harm unless provoked."

He shifted slightly, the harsh glow of the sun-mimicking lamps casting deep shadows across his face.

"Like the plants it resembles, it draws its energy from sunlight. That's how it survives, feeding on light itself."

John's eyes never left the creature. His voice cut through the sterile hum of the chamber.

"Then tell me," he said coldly, "how does a shy and passive thing tear a poor man to pieces?"

The director shifted his stance, his gaze steady as he raised a hand and pointed toward the creature's torso.

"Look there," he said.

John and Varun's eyes followed his gesture. On the creature's right chest and lower abdomen, the bark-like flesh was marred by two gaping wounds. They weren't fresh, but deep, ragged hollows that bore the unmistakable shape of bullet impacts.

What made the sight unsettling was not the wounds themselves, but what filled them now. From the dark cavities sprouted patches of moss and tender green shoots, slowly weaving over the damage as though it was knitting the creature back together.

"It was shot that night," the director said, his voice calm but edged with something heavier. "Wounded... desperate. It managed to kill two of the men who attacked it before it fled."

He paused, his gaze shifting to Varun. For a moment, the room felt colder.

"Your father was truly unfortunate," the director continued quietly. "He stumbled across it while it was hurt and panicked. Wrong place... wrong time."

Varun's jaw tightened as he stared at the creature. His fists clenched. John placed a steady hand on his shoulder, grounding him.

"But how did it tear a man limb from limb? It doesn't look that strong," John asked, his tone sharp.

The director's eyes flicked to the dormant figure.

"Telekinesis," he said simply. "We don't fully understand it yet... but it can move things with its mind. That's how we believe it killed your father." He leaned back slightly, his voice lowering. "It also emits bursts of electromagnetic pulses. Enough to fry electronics, cameras, even some weapons. That's why it's been so difficult to track and contain."

He let out a slow breath, his expression heavy. "I am truly sorry, Varun. We all are. But you must understand, it was an accident."

"Accident...?" Varun's voice cracked, anger flaring in his eyes. "You people shot it, and then it killed my father. This is your fault!"

The director shook his head firmly. "No, Mr. Varun. We didn't shoot it."

John's eyes narrowed. "Then who did?"

The director hesitated, his face darkening. "That is still a mystery. Its existence... leaked. Outsiders came hunting for it. We don't know who they were. That night, it was attacked, wounded... and then your father crossed its path." His voice lowered as he glanced back at the dormant creature. "After that, it entered this hibernation state. We believe it's healing itself. And this" he gestured to the chamber, the lights, the glass "this is the first time we've ever had it under our control. Until now, we could only observe it in the wild. If there was one good thing to come from that night... it's this."

The director's gaze lingered on Varun, steady but weighed with sorrow.

"And the two people responsible for this..." his voice lowered, carrying a grim finality, "...had a more brutal fate than your father. Believe me, Mr. Varun."

He glanced toward the creature, his expression haunted. "When it struck them, it wasn't quick, and it wasn't merciful. By the time we reached the site, there was nothing left but blood and fragments of bone scattered through the trees. Whatever this thing is... it doesn't forgive when it's cornered."

He let the silence hang in the sterile room, the humming of machines filling the space where his words could not. "Your father..." he continued more quietly, almost as if trying to convince himself, "...your father's death, as terrible as it was, might have been the kinder end."

John slowly draped an arm across Varun's shoulder, grounding him, keeping him steady. Varun's eyes, however, never left the creature.

The director's voice softened, almost hesitant now.

"You seeing your father's body... that became a problem for us. Then the police became involved, and suddenly there was too much attention. We couldn't afford the public learning what really happened out there."

He paused, the weight of his words pressing down on the sterile chamber. His gaze flickered briefly to the floor before finding Varun again.

"That's why we called it a tiger attack. That's why we buried the truth. I am... sorry, Varun."

Varun's gaze lingered on the creature, his chest rising and falling in uneven breaths as though each exhale was forcing the grief out of him. Slowly, painfully, he steadied himself, like a man who had finally found the answer he both longed for and dreaded. His fists unclenched, but his eyes stayed on the being that had unraveled his world.

"Come with me," the director said at last, his tone clipped but quieter than before. He turned, already striding toward the door.

John gave Varun a reassuring pat on the back and guided him forward. Together they followed the director, the soldier A7 falling into step behind them like a shadow that refused to leave.

***

The chamber sealed shut with a heavy hiss. At once, jets of sterilizing mist sprayed down, cloaking them in a cold, chemical fog. The soldier A7 stood just behind John and Varun.

The door ahead unlocked with a metallic click, sliding open. One by one, attendants helped peel away the weight of the hazmat suits. The director shrugged his off with practiced ease, while John and Varun wrestled against the heavy fabric until they were free, their breaths lighter. The soldier A7, shed his suit last.

The next door slid open with a muted hiss, and the director stepped out without a word. John and Varun trailed behind him, their footsteps echoing softly against the sterile floor.

He led them down the corridor, turned sharply at the corner, and keyed open another door.

Inside was a room that immediately felt different from the rest of the facility. A personal office.

John's eyes roamed curiously. A single framed photograph rested on the desk– the director standing beside Dr. A.P.J. Abdul Kalam, both smiling in a rare captured moment. Beside it sat a sleek laptop, its screen dark, wires neatly arranged. The room had no windows, no glimpse of the outside world, but the steady hum of hidden vents kept the air flowing cool and controlled.

The director moved with calm precision, lowering himself into the chair behind the desk. He gestured toward the seats opposite him.

"Sit," he said simply.

John and Varun settled into the chairs, facing him across the polished surface.In the corner, the soldier A7 took his place against the wall, standing like a silent sentinel.

"So now you know the truth," the director said, his tone firm but weary. "And it is time for you both to keep your side of the deal. From this moment on, neither of you should speak of this to anyone."

"Sure," John replied without hesitation.

"We won't speak about it."

The director's gaze shifted to Varun.

"And you?"

Varun swallowed, his eyes drifting briefly toward the memory of the creature behind the chamber doors.

"Me too. I just wanted to know the truth... that's it. I won't tell anyone."

The director leaned back slightly, exhaling through his nose as though satisfied. Then, after a pause, he glanced at John again.

"And the girl?"

John frowned. "The girl?" His voice carried confusion, almost defensiveness.

"What was her name, A7?" the director asked, turning to the soldier as though recalling a detail he shouldn't have forgotten.

"Priya," A7 said flatly, his voice devoid of emotion, as if reciting a fact from a file.

"How do you know? Wait..." John's eyes narrowed. "You bugged the house."

The director's lips curved into a small, knowing smile. "Sharp as ever. Yes, we needed to keep tabs on you."

John's jaw tightened, but before he could say more, the director shifted his gaze. "So... will she be a problem?"

"No," John said firmly. "She doesn't know much, and it will stay that way."

"That's good," the director replied, his smile fading into something colder. "But remember this, I will be watching both of you. Don't mistake my kindness for weakness. I don't want more trouble spilling into my operations. I already have enough problems to deal with." His eyes lingered on them, heavy with warning.

"Are we all on the same page?"

"Yes," both John and Varun said at the same time.

"Well, that is good to hear." The director leaned forward, extending his hand. He shook theirs firmly, one by one, before easing back into his chair. A faint smile touched his lips.

"It was a pleasure meeting you both."

He leaned back in his chair, perfectly at ease.

"Please," he said softly, almost kindly. "Have some tea... or water. It will help with the dizziness when you wake up."

"Dizziness?" John repeated, a crease forming on his brow.

That was when he noticed A7 was already behind them. Silent. Too silent. John hadn't heard a single step.

The soldier moved with mechanical precision. In one fluid motion, the needle slid into John's shoulder. He gasped, trying to react, but A7 had already turned to Varun. The second injection came just as quick, efficient, cold.

John's vision swam, the edges of the room dissolving. He forced his gaze to the director, clinging to consciousness for a final moment.

The director's faint smile never faltered.

"It was nice meeting you, Mr. John," he said calmly, as though bidding farewell to a guest. "Let's hope... this was our last meeting."

CHAPTER 9

Farwell

John's eyes flickered open. His head throbbed, each beat of his pulse hammering behind his temples. For a moment, he didn't recognize where he was, then the familiar ceiling came into focus. Varun's house. His bed.

He pushed himself upright slowly, his body heavy, his mind foggy. Instinctively, he reached for his phone on the side table. It wasn't there. *They must have taken it,* he thought grimly.

A dry rasp burned in his throat. That's when he noticed it, on the table beside him, a bottle of water, neatly placed. It hadn't been there before. He froze, unease knotting in his gut. Next to it lay his pistol, polished clean, the weight of it more unsettling than reassuring.

He stared for a long moment, suspicion gnawing at him. Then, with a slow breath, he reached for the bottle, unscrewed the cap, and drank. The water was cool, refreshing.

His eyes flicked back to the pistol. *Did they leave it as a courtesy or as a message?*

John stood, steadying himself, and stepped into the hallway. Varun's door was open; he peeked in to see his friend sprawled on the bed, still unconscious, breathing steadily. Relief washed over him.

In the living room, the clock ticked steadily. 2:00 PM. They had been out for hours.

John moved to the main door and unlatched it. To his surprise, the lock had been fixed, repaired perfectly, as though it had never been broken. Another *courtesy* from the director, he realized, his jaw tightening.

The world felt unsettlingly normal. Rain had washed the streets clean that morning, leaving the scent of wet earth in the air. Near the porch, Varun's motorbike stood parked, waiting silently, as though nothing had happened.

Outside, near the steps, John noticed two of Priya's familiar steel food containers stacked neatly with a folded note resting on top. He bent down, picked it up, and unfolded the paper.

"Let me know if you are going out."

A faint smile tugged at John's lips. Even in the middle of everything, Priya still managed to be thoughtful. He carried the containers inside and set them on the dining table. His stomach growled the moment the smell of food hit him.

Crossing the hall, he stepped into Varun's room and gently shook his shoulder.

"Wake up," John said softly.

Varun stirred, eyes heavy. John handed him the bottle of water.

"Drink this. Come on, let's eat, you must be starving."

A few minutes later, the two of them washed up and sat at the dining table. For the first time since the ordeal, there was something almost normal about the moment, warm food between them, the silence of the house, and Priya's containers like a small reminder of safety.

It was rice, fish fry, and sambar inside the containers. They sat down and began eating.

"Do you have your phone? I think they took mine," Varun said between bites.

"Yeah... mine too," John replied.

Varun hesitated. "So it's over, right, sir?"

John looked at him steadily. "I hope so. If we keep our mouths shut, everything will be fine."

"Are they... watching us still?" Varun asked, his voice lower now.

John's eyes instinctively swept the room, scanning the corners, the ceiling, the walls, searching for anything out of place. "Maybe... maybe not. Not sure," he admitted.

There was a pause. The clinking of plates and the hum of the afternoon outside filled the silence.

"Now you know the truth," John finally said, "what are you going to do next?"

Varun sighed, staring at his plate. "I don't know, sir. I think I need to leave this place for a while. Clear my head. Maybe travel, explore a bit. Come back when my mind feels right."

John nodded approvingly. "Good. That's good, Varun. If you ever pass through Trivandrum, come see me."

"Sure, sir," Varun said with a faint smile.

***

When John had finished eating, he washed his hands and returned to Varun's side. "I'll start packing. Can you drop me at the bus stop?"

"You're leaving?" Varun asked, almost startled.

"The task is done. My part here is over," John said simply.

Varun's expression softened. "Okay... there's a bus at 3:30. I'll take you then."

"Perfect."

John went into the room and packed his belongings, his wallet, his clothes, his pistol, all neatly back into his backpack. When he stepped out, Varun was waiting, holding a bundle of cash in his hands. He smiled nervously and offered it forward.

"This is twenty thousand. I don't know your fee, but... if this is less, I'll send the rest to your account later."

John smiled faintly and pushed his hand back. "No need, son. You've given me an experience of a lifetime. That's payment enough. Keep the money, rebuild your life. That's worth more."

Varun's eyes welled with tears. He hugged John tightly, and John returned the embrace with quiet strength. After a few moments, they pulled apart, Varun quickly wiping his face with his sleeve.

They stepped outside. The air smelled damp from the morning rain. Varun locked the house, pushed his bike through the gate, and held it steady. As he was about to climb on, John asked, "Hey, mind if I ride this time?"

Varun blinked, then smiled. "Sure."

John swung his leg over, handing his bag to Varun. Once Varun settled on the back, John started the bike. The engine growled to life, and together, they rode off down the wet road, the forest watching silently around them.

They rode in silence, the hum of the bike filling the space between them. Neither spoke a word as the road wound past the turn toward the deep forest, the place of the crime, the old *kavu*, the shadows that now held their darkest answers. The trees seemed to watch them as they passed, ancient and unmoving, like silent witnesses to secrets best left buried.

The forest thinned, giving way to the familiar bustle of the town. Soon, the bike slowed near the Kallukad bus stop. Varun climbed off as John eased the bike to the side of the road and killed the engine.

"It's been a while since I rode a bike," John said, swinging his leg over and pulling his backpack from Varun's hands.

The bus was waiting at the stop, engine rumbling. John hugged Varun one last time. For a fleeting moment, he felt as though he were saying goodbye to a son.

"Take care. Don't get into any trouble," John said. "Tell Priya I'm leaving. She's a good girl. And if you're ever near Trivandrum, don't forget to call me, alright?"

"Okay, sir." Varun replied.

John patted his shoulder with a faint smile.

"Not sir. Just John. Goodbye."

"Goodbye," Varun said, waving as John climbed onto the bus.

Through the dusty window, John caught one last glimpse of Varun standing at the roadside, hand lifted in farewell until distance blurred him from sight.

Kallukad slipped away behind him, a place of secrets and shadows, now part of his past. The weathered sign at the edge of town swayed in the wind, its faded letters offering a final farewell:

"Thanks, come back again. – Kallukad"

John leaned back, closed his eyes, and let the road take him away.

www.ingramcontent.com/pod-product-compliance
Lightning Source LLC
Chambersburg PA
CBHW050017170726
48282CB00025B/439
* 9 7 8 9 3 3 4 4 2 1 3 4 7 *